THE THEORY OF LIGHT AT MIDNIGHT

the
THEORY
of LIGHT
AT MIDNIGHT
ELIZABETH
UKRAINETZ

TIGHTROPE BOOKS

2015

Tightrope Books
#207—2 College Street, Toronto, ON M5G 1K3
www.tightropebooks.com

Editor: Marnie Woodrow
Copy editor: Vera DeWaard
Cover design: Deanna Janovski
Typography: Carleton Wilson
Author photo: Kye Marshall

We thank the Canada Council for the Arts and the Ontario Arts
Council for their support of our publishing program.

ONTARIO ARTS COUNCIL
CONSEIL DES ARTS DE L'ONTARIO
an Ontario government agency
un organisme du gouvernement de l'Ontario

Canada Council   Conseil des Arts
for the Arts   du Canada

Printed and bound in Canada

Library and Archives Canada Cataloguing in Publication

Ukrainetz, Elizabeth, author
The theory of light at midnight / Elizabeth Ukrainetz.

ISBN 978-1-926639-86-4 (paperback)

I. Title.

PS8591.K73T44 2015   C813'.54   C2015-903666-6

For my family
And for Barb & Linda,
Jennifer & Maureen

"Why do you let such cowardice sleep in your heart?"

Dante

ONE

Abstraction is an asylum from tragedy

I don't know if violence has meaning, but that it has profound effect I am almost certain. Of what I had remembered of the first assault—not the assault on me but on another girl—was only the image of her as we found her, a girl's body tied up under the bridge, left for dead. I had forgotten everything around it, the before and after, the entire year around it. Except for the image of her, an inexplicable fear of bridges and heights, and night dreams of climbing endless black sliding muck.

Wandering late summer grade school, and Max saw her first; harshly stopped short, mouth gasping silent under the flop of his black hair, wordless, pointing up to the shadows under the railway overpass. The image burnt into my mind; the intricate black lacework of the girdings against the sky, the parallel lengths of railway tracks, *black-blue black-blue black-blue* splicing straight through the lace. I sighted the line of the tracks, searched the lacework, the regular lumps where things connect and, there, between the first and second pylon, there she was a soft round lump, animal-shaped, against the lattice. The shadow of the missing girl.

We started crawling up the side of the ravine, clutching rocks and branches, pulling our bodies up and forward, slipping at every second step, bashing ourselves against the slope to get to her. At the top of the ravine the track headed into the air. I could see the loops of the heavy ropes snaked around the planks in two places, holding the body in place. The tracks beamed out across the sky on heavy stilts through the empty air. Far below, the river swirled in green and white pillowed currents. I stepped on the first railway tie and the world shifted sideways, knocking me back to the edge of the ravine. Rectangles of white gravel between each wooden slat, long grass and wild flowers dry and sharp in the late summer sun.

I took a deep breath and started crawling forward, knee by knee, hand by hand, the sky above, the river below, this thin rail and her body in between, crawling forward until I reached the spot just above her.

"Girl," I said. "Girl?"

There was no answer.

The river below, a gurgle and a whisper, constant as the sky.

The sky, a high wide plane, sheer and empty.

The image burnt into my mind, slipping there always, in day dream, night dream, reaching. As for the captivity when I was twelve, and what happened after, the space where I did remember was as blank as this sky.

Canadian Pastoral

We are in the car, Louis and me, heading out to Penetan-guishene. The road is fast and wet. I sit back in the red bucket seat, determined to rest my head, my body, as Louis zips past car after car after truck, zipping in and out, behind, in front, using the slow lanes to pass cars that don't move over quickly enough. Bumper seems to skim bumper, touch for a breath, then pass. It is a jour-ney of narrow escapes. We've never had an accident, but my knuckles clutch the upholstery the whole way, my feet jerk to non-existent brakes. The highway slides under our wheels safe, hard, rolling along. Coming out of Toronto along Highway 401 to the 400 we pass over, and under, overpass after overpass, the curved construc-tion of metal, cement, and asphalt arcing in light curves against the grid streets of the city. I hold my breath tight at each one, unable to not check the shadows under the grids for the shape of a body, a girl.

An hour out of town the highway clears, few cars and no overpasses, and I relax. If we spin out now, we won't kill anyone else. It'll just be us. Louis relaxes, too, away from the video game he supposes driving to be, into a musical musing state, big body slouched into an *ess*, lightly rooted to the gas pedal, cedar-brown hair flopped forward, pushed back, flopped forward. Eyes blank to the road.

Grains of asphalt appear out of the blend of distance, melding into speed, and the landscape opens up into flat white fields spotted with lines of wind-break trees, a gentle roll with hills and haze and marsh. Penetanguishene comes faster than I expect, the highway slowing into the main street of the town, dipping and stopping at the lip of the frozen harbour, an almost perfect circle, dotted with ice fishing huts and Ski-Doos.

Louis pulls into a gas station just before Robert Street, gets out of the car with a clunk and a slam of the door. Sitting as he fills the tank, the sun glints off the gas station window so I can see my reflection, my face, the car in the glass, adjust my vision to see the guy inside at the cash, two guys leaning against the counter smoking and talking. I follow one man's body down to the bottom edge of the window where four newspaper boxes are lined up, their headlines variations on the same event: the limbs of a young woman, a teenage girl, found along the shore west of Toronto, encased in crumbling concrete, shredded plastic, unidentifiable.

A rush of cold air rushes into the warm car.

Do you want coffee, Magda?

Sure.

The text of the headlines blurs, disappears, as we pull away, bend into the snow-covered curves of a country road, barely losing speed. I know he drives best, superbly, only in crisis; that he needs to create this level of danger in order to maintain the keen alertness that keeps us safe. This is his balancing act. The road slides, curved. He glances a quick side-glance at me, and I just shake my head.

"Do you actually know where we're going?"

"Oh, yeah. Been there a million times."

"Ten years ago."

"This isn't Toronto. They don't move buildings and trees around like tents and circuses."

The road clears of houses, becomes all pine bough, thick and sharp. Forest. We continue on the fresh fallen ground, into real forest, beautiful in deep winter. Louis slows, bends forward over the steering wheel, searching.

"I think. It's right…" he stops in front of an anonymous piece of snow bank, "here."

"Here?" I say, looking at the blank wall of snow that stretches back and forward as far as I can see, indistinguishable.

He puts the car in gear, pulls the emergency brake up, snaps off the engine, hops out, opens the trunk, then my door.

"Here," he says, pushing a shovel into my hand.

"Dig us in, girl."

The snow is weightless. Untouched for days, it lifts into the scoop of the shovel and flies before falling in a peaked pile by the driveway. I take it in three easy layers, moving down to the asphalt metre-square by metre-square. It's easy work, intoxicating in the clean northern air, a relief to my urban bones. And quiet work, the slight rasp of the shovel a breath beside my own.

When I met Louis five years ago, I was keeping my life busy but often couldn't sleep so I'd go out for late-night walks, three or four in the morning, throw on a big sweater, and walk until my legs felt like cement. Bay and Queen unlit. Jarvis and Sherbourne after the bars are long closed and the hookers and johns had gone home. I heard him before I saw him: a sharp sweet sound, moan on the edge of a wail, barely heard but there, disappearing with the wind or the odd taxi. I made my way toward the sound: sweeping high and low, block by block, quick and slow. And it was Louis, standing at the abandoned corner of Yonge and Bloor in the useless glimmer of neon light, playing his violin in an alcove while the light snow melted a few feet from the ground. I stopped where I was, captured, listening, until he saw me too, and nodded and played, he said, until his fingertips were raw.

For months he met me after work, walking me home through the sidewalk crowd. He talked and talked, explaining how the binary at the base of computers is the essence of human consciousness, the yin and yang, darkness and light, working right though without *chi*, without mystery, animation. There has to be a third, he says, a third element that remains unknown. On hot days he brought ice cream or smoothies. Cold days he brought me his gloves; they fit loose over my hands, my fingers curled into fists as we walked. He taught me symphony, Chinatown, Little India, Little Italy; taught me Bergman, Kurosawa, Fellini. The edge of this culture touched my awareness, began to tilt me into something that felt, then, like substance: huge, complex, subtle, sensible. He walks, he runs, he dances, and I follow. His eyes are shining, his body is moving, and I shine and move, run and dance behind.

Love can be like this. It can be a submission of trust, of faith, in another's love. It can be the self submitted and erased and re-made in the eyes of another, reconstructed from their dreams and expectations.

I stop shoveling at the end of the driveway, slouch against the fence, and the silence begins to take shape, size. My breath quiets in the still air and the non-sound of winter seeps into me, slow, still deep, then it reaches out, spreading into the snow, the sky, boundless. I hear a light breeze, snow tapping on the vinyl of my parka, my breath then, my pulse.

White clumped pine and cedar line the rectangle of the log fence. Snow drifts up to the edges of their bottom branches in a sharp wave around the yard. Rabbit tracks close to the trees, shadows spooned in the white. The shallow scrawl of bird tracks barely visible. I've made an edge at the gate that reaches my thighs. A crow caws and is answered. Scanning the tree tops for its perch, I spin and tip, fall backward, hear the soft thud of the shovel as I land into softness, feel the stuff come perfectly around me, holding me there, molding as I landed. I fold my hands over my chest and breathe into the white sky, feel my body heat in the snow, then the cold, seeping gently up through my clothes.

The glass of wine in my hand is warm and red, in a short, wide-mouthed tumbler. The cottage faces a spectacular view of the islands and bay, frozen solid and white into every distance, the white sky barely discernable as a separate mass. I've put on sunglasses to look out, trying to conceive the idea of the reality my senses are giving me, to absorb it as real. 'God's green earth', I think, but it's white, sheer white, and sheer ice, so barren of contour that I can, I think, see forever, sheer north.

Way out on the flat, ant-specks of people ski or Ski-Doo across the bay, moving in a swift glide from land to island to fishing hole, the mechanics of their movements lost with distance.

Louis practices in the back bedroom, Vivaldi, Haydn, then flips into a Cajun jig, turning a violin into a fiddle with the lift of an elbow, crossing centuries and cultures in a beat. He'll be out soon.

Louis left school when he was sixteen to program computers. Early days. He worked day and night on synthesized music, living off Big Macs and KitKats, turning his parent's basement into a living animal of wires and nodes, disembodied keyboards standing on tube metal legs; flat white fingers, skinny black thumbs, reaching from a den of wires that clumped and tangled and clumped, spreading across the room, up the walls, to another keyboard, a CPU, a monitor. Only he knew what led to what, the subtleties of connection—here across the room, the green wire to the black, red to yellow; we'll try it that way and if it doesn't work, I'll take the red and the green, pull them across the room to the four orange at the motherboard, solder and trace a pathway, then the fifth orange comes to the black at the base of the monitor, and the brown, the brown goes…

He never dreamed that it was lust, passion that drove him to the work. He'd laugh if I suggested it now, contemptuous. But it was lust. Not lust for wires but lust for a girl, Sarah, who sat in front of him, two rows over, in Chemistry on Mondays; three seats ahead in English on Thursdays. She wore her hair back with a band, the black of the cloth against her brown hair, curving behind her ear, the curve of her jaw arcing lightly to her chin, her lips. And curving down, too, her neck, her chest, the scoop of her sweater. The thump of his dreams waking him into sweat.

That's when the work began, when he quit school, went into the basement and then he couldn't leave the work even for an hour. If he left the work, even for twenty minutes, the soul would fall out of the project, all the wires would fall, become a mess rather than an idea. He did it once, left the work for an hour and a half to do his dad's income tax. All the numbers there, instructions, take the amount from line 32 and place it on line 65, subtract 10% of line 29 from line 65, if you are not claiming a credit from Supplemental Form D7. There's a system, thought, some basic idea that must underlie the reasoning. Take the amount from D7-19. When he stepped back down into the basement, it was gone. The soul was gone from the machine. He sat down in the middle of the nest of wires, sat down, emptied, too, of soul, blinking into the tangle of tangles, sitting, waiting, blinking, following one wire then the next for days, nights, until they all attached again, came alive, breathing idea and method and question into the pulsing basement. He hadn't moved an inch of muscle against the air, hadn't touched a thing, and it came back.

He didn't talk to anyone after that, so terrified was he at the near-death, until, two years later, when all the beeps and bass, trumpets and squeals had been blinking the air for eleven months and he thought: this is not music.

The work collapsed into filament, node, plastic and metal, a natural death. He trudged up the basement stairs, light-footed, blinked into the bright kitchen. Saw his father sitting on the deck with a book, took two beers out of the fridge. He popped a cap off as he sat down with his dad. Flies buzzed at the corner of the step. His dad nodded to the tree in the corner of the yard, "The magnolias are blooming." Louis was twenty-one. He chugged the first beer, opened the second, and decided to learn the violin.

"Hey—I like the shades."

"I need them!" I say, nodding toward the blinding landscape. "I'd be blind in ten minutes without them."

"Then don't look." He kisses the back of my neck.

"Can't help it," I turn and kiss his mouth.

He takes my glass.

"Wow—that guy's really moving"

A skier zips at an angle across the ice, barely a dot but near enough that we can see his arms pumping quick, poles dipping into the snow then flying behind, skis cutting a sharp line across the bay.

"Looks like he knows where he's going."

"He's sure moving. Makes me hungry just watching."

"Is there food here?"

"Ah-hum."

He places his palms flat against the back of my neck and bites. His body comes close behind me, pressed, he slips each hand under the neck of my sweater, pushing my shoulders bare. I lean backward into his chest, my butt nudging his crotch. His hands cross under my bra, arms wrapped around my shoulders as he leans us forward, my cheek and breasts on the window, cold. I reach back behind us, clutch the thick loose denim, pushing his hips into me. His arm across my torso, hand cupped between my legs, we move, rhythm, squirm against each other and the glass. I move against him, match move to move, scrambling in memory and mind for arousal, for an image, a response that is deeper than the skin, deeper than the warm comfort of his body beside mine, deeper than the knowledge of his desire. In the end I fall back on reflecting his desire back to him, expert now at pulling the force of his desire to peak and ebb and peak, distracting him from the absence of my pleasure to the heat of his.

I understand that there is a place where he goes, where people go, where I have not been. I feel it as a physical deformity, the absence of a limb or an eye. What is it that pulled men to me, that chained women to men—that pushes them through their lives. I do not know how it feels in the heart, in the body, to be filled, consumed, blissed, taken over, filled up. I've seen it in so many bodies, and I do not know what it is: what happens to them as they desire and arouse and peak; that sweeps them away so entirely, takes them so far away, from caring about anything or anyone around. What is it to go inside like that, to let go and not die.

I feel only the surface waves of actions. I had felt the edge of some hunger, some mania, once, but even in that intensity it never reached my sex, my body. Just longing, bottomless longing, and the comfort of feeling whole while I was with him; Dana, long gone. Louis is familiar, and so comfortable, but there has never been a longing.

I scrounge my mind for the image of a breast, a dick, some movie scrap of intensity, sensation, to drag a response from my thighs. We move against each other, crouching with our clothes to the floor. I wet him, then myself. He moves into me in the strange light of the reflected snow.

There is a body strung out across the ravine at the top of Eighth Street, hard rope tightening around ankles and wrists, calves and shoulders stretched to arch and straining, joint loosening from joint as she hangs there, suspended between the two sides.

Branches are bending, roots loosening from the soil, big brown centipedes scampering away, mice leaving home.

In the north sky a falcon soars, catching wind-drift to glide.

Forty feet below, the river streams south, trout and tadpoles flick and twitch around rocks, grass, and weeds.

There is a wind. A slight sway. A slight awakening.

Deer nibble at leaves, follow the green from the woods to the river's edge and along the shore. Squirrels chirrup from high branches, tails cranking in fear. Chipmunks dart and hop from underbrush to clearing and under, nibbling at roots. The subway passes a mile up the ravine, its rumble, taken into the ground, passes from layer to layer, diminishing.

It was supposed to be a tag, a rag, something to do to kill an evening. And this it did.

Suspended from earth to earth, the body becomes fire, then stone. The neck comes unjointed, the smallest vertebrae, simple pebbles holding the biggest weight, loosen and the head hangs backward, full down, hinged from the body. We are weight.

The spine elongates, rib pulls away from rib, small arcs stretching wide inside the chest, trachea pulled long. Organ leaves organ and the tiny connecting tubes thin out. The body, its breath and movement and thought, becomes stone.

How ridiculous to place a stone here, at the centre of air, in the middle of emptiness. How foolish.

Placed in this position, it is your own body that undoes you, the sharpness of a bone, the thinness of the skin, the weight you didn't lose last summer and the reasons you never ran track, worked out at the gym.

There is a rope, there is a girl, there is a rope.

Ten kilometres away my family sits at the Thanksgiving meal listening to television and country music. Everyone laughs at the baby and Mom jumps up to get more potatoes.

Fifty kilometres away Louis takes the elevator up thirty-six storeys of the darkened building, finds his way through the corridors by the red glow of the exit lights, opens the fuse box and lights half a floor.

A thousand kilometres away Sarah catches a midday plane from Brussels to Paris, stopping over for a few days on her way to London.

A few blocks away Max, black hair tangled into grey, crawls deeper between the bench and the building, pulling crisp leaves and wrappers closer around his feet and hands.

Half a world away, after forty-three years, a survivor un-survives, throwing himself four storeys deep. Safe. Gone.

General Linguistics

We trudge across the ice, past the end of the rocks and the pier into the blank sheet of cold, moving slow and steady in a direct line across the bay where James and Sarah have invited the gang for a winter bonfire. The afternoon is warm and clear, icicles dripping, daylight already lengthening from the solstice. The sun is on my face, sinking in the western sky. I try to get the feel of the earth turning away from the sun, the scientific fact of it, but perception is stronger than knowledge, we do not turn and the sun sinks down. Snow is thick and wet on my boots, walking through snow, on snow and ice thick enough to hold a line of snowmobiles, a crowd of men in fishing huts. And water, then. Water. And sleepy-brained fish.

Louis' red jacket ahead. In the distance a green, a blue, a black jacket, other people moving in from other shores. We are so small here, bodies creeping across a landscape made of relentless distance. My eyes ache with the light, the white so bright, the ice so far, the trudge of feet beading the top snow into grain. Louis waits and we wrap an arm around each other. His breath comes onto my face. Our jackets crumple into each other, thick, insulating from warmth as well as cold.

> (I was twelve when I was kidnapped and kept in a
> cell in the basement of a basement. I remember
> the smell of dirt and the sound of screams falling

into darkness. Buried there, I remember the darkness as warmth, peace.)

Within a circle of snow we sit around the fire, jackets open to the heat, night surrounding, cold at our backs. Crackle of wood, clank of beer, and hot potatoes, roasted in foil at the foot of the fire, broken open, lusty crust into steaming white. Songs have been sung, animals consumed. We are leaning into each other and the fire. Across the fire, James breaks the circle, facing away, his back hunched over an open cooler, the pry and scrape of his shucking knife grates the air as he fills a plate with oysters. Sarah moves to lean over him, her face buried in the shadow of his lean. I imagine a heat from their bodies, a glow, hear something wet and turn back to the fire. Louis slips a hand under my jacket, down the back of my snow suit. The plate goes around, a little lemon, a little Tabasco, the slime and rush of the sea in my throat, breaking the lull of heat and cold, rousing the others to leave. Me and Sarah start picking up bottles, plates.

"Leave them. Leave them," Louis says. "They're empty."

Heading inside with two bottles of red.

"Useless," he says.

He throws an arm around Sarah, "C'mon, girls."

"That is, without a doubt, the most ridiculous thing I have ever heard."

Sarah grabs another bottle of wine, refills glasses all around. She's in the second year of her Master's in Cultural Studies. The arguments are fierce: right and wrong; capture of subtlety, nuance, the shade of meaning into understanding. Her language has become full, words that stretch blocks and hold houses of meanings. Complex. Loaded. Or—she doesn't see—simply an impenetrable mass of badly named abstractions. Her mother doesn't understand her anymore, her old friends don't understand. She thinks this is because she knows something, or is on the brink of knowing something, that they aren't able to grasp, but sometimes, late at night when she's hit a dead end at the curve of an essay or when she's taking the long bus ride to the campus and forgotten her books, the lull of the bus, the geography passing, sometimes in these moments she thinks maybe this isn't true at all, that she's not on the brink of anything. The edge of the thought barely surfaces because as soon as it does, she breaks out in a sweat, terror, her pulse leaps up to 120 in a flash, and she starts thinking again, riding the lollygag of words in their spin. *Saussure, Saussure, took a thought and caused a stir.* Near-rhyme. Near-rhyme. Which is an act of the tongue, the throat. The shape of the ear and its parts. The brain firing synapses that shape sound into something commonly heard. Understood.

She glances at me and James before fixing Louis over the rim of her glass. He's been keeping up, reading her books page for page, following names into libraries, articles, papers.

"And what is it that is so ridiculous that you've never heard the like in your oh-so-vast life?"

"An object," he pauses while he sips.

"An object cannot be a sign. It is, by nature, an object. The thing itself. Not the sign for a thing. A sign is. Inherently. Empty."

Sarah and James are Louis's oldest friends. When he came out of the basement, he got a job at MacDonald's, beside the bookstore on Yonge Street. When he took his breaks, went out in the alley for a smoke, James was there, taking a break from the bookstore. They got to talking. James plays harmonica, accordion, piano, so they took to practicing together, then making lunch money by playing evenings on the street at the corner of Bloor and Cumberland, College and Yonge. When James brought his girl—she'd been away for a year, in London, not to visit the Queen but to visit the Slade where she studied photography and sound—Louis recognized her from somewhere but couldn't place her. Sarah didn't recognize him at all. On nights when they went out to the Horseshoe, Grossman's, the El Mocombo, when the band was playing bluegrass, country, jazz or rock, she'd catch him looking, and she'd smile, knocking him out of his wondering. He'd shake his head, shrug. Somewhere, he'd say, somewhere; near-re-membrance an ache in his belly, a loneliness building. He left them at the corner of Queen, walking east while he trudged north, hauling his violin like a small coffin at this hour, in this mood, up the slope of Yonge to Bloor, where the acoustics of wind carried the sublime screech and whine—assonance, dissonance—from corner to corner, brick to brick to concrete slab, deepening, muffling, shaping the sound off walls and corners, billboards and hollow doorways, then up where it wandered, east, north, west, south to the lapping lake and the wide stretch of air where no building was, no foot or hand or belly aching.

Louis swigs down his glass.

"It has to be empty in order to be a sign, otherwise it's an object itself and an object has its own meaning, its own existence, which cannot be contained within a sign. A sign is a simplification. It's something that points to an object. An object can't point to itself. That—" he pours another glass "— would be ridiculous."

"An object can't point to itself?" She lifts her glass, "How many drinks have *you* had?"

"No. Unless it's a sign. Then it becomes the object *sign*. That's not what we're talking about."

"Listen. The external form of the whole object becomes a sign for the object, as well as the object itself, so an object can be a sign of itself as well as itself."

"Like tomatoes."

"What?" Sarah and Louis look at James. He tips back in his chair, his eyes closed, glass balanced on his belly.

"The ones you buy at Loblaws now. They aren't real tomatoes. They have no tomato-ness. No taste. No smell. No colour."

"Sometimes colour," I say.

James squints his eyes open, nods. "Sometimes colour. But in and of themselves, they are not tomatoes but a sign of what a tomato would be if you could get one. A big, round, wet, sign."

"But aren't they just a different type of tomato? Real Tomato."

"Ah. Type. Genus."

"Say, genetically. They are 'Tomato.'"

"And not just *tomato* itself."

Sarah looks at Louis, "What are you guys talking about?"

"We are talking about," James untips his chair, "it's late and we want to go to bed."

Affliction

Back in the city a warm day turns winter into slush, soaking my legs as I slog home after work, pick up books and
clothes and head to Louis' house. The streetcar screeches
Carlton into Parliament, packed with rush hour. Watching rhythms from the window, there is something here,
in the shape of our streets and our houses and snow falling so thick across it all, that resonates. People trudge
bundled up on the street, wearing black coats and red
scarves, heavy boots gridding the salted slush, going
about the business of their daily lives; walking blocks
for this particular bread, that particular cheese, meeting
friends for coffee when their own cupboards are full,
their kitchens warm; going in and out of shops as if it
were the mildest spring day, risking the slide of slipping
asphalt to fulfill their routine. Something in this. Yearn-
ing. Warmth.

I slip off at the Goodwill, walk a street, a corner,
through a little black iron gate. His hallway is the size of
my apartment. Polished slate tiles, deep green. Louis is
home, or he is not home. There is a fire, or there is no
fire. The dining room, heavy oak, jade and white. Wide
stairs curling up the side of the walls, one floor, two floor,
three. Arced triptych of windows, stained-glass peonies
lifting pink tip and green leaf into amber.

At the kitchen counter I unload my books, spread
them out and open the world of academics, ideas; a
world, it seems to me, that has no end. Darting off in

all directions, going off forever, stopping abruptly for a turn left, right, up, down; densely populated, rich, packed with detail and opinion, observation and idea. The breakdown of experience into parts and wholes and parts, configured, disputed and re-configured. Identification, distinction, formulation. My mind dives into this, flies into this, handstand and swan dive, waterslide and belly flops from the high board; caught, anyway, by voices, human voices; crowds of people walking through, living their lives, speaking their minds, listening, looking. Leaving notes, paragraphs, books. I take my own notes, underline, highlight, word, thought, concept, try to listen well.

The front door opens a draft around my legs.

"I'm in here."

He shuffles in, all posture gone, bends over my shoulders, his coat opening me in.

"What are you working on?"

"Shamanism. Siberia."

"Ah—Tree of Life. Bone stock. That sort of thing?"

"Exactly that."

"Have you got Eliade? He did the ground work for hallucinogens."

"The horse-pee-ecstasy stuff?" I prop the book closed to show the cover.

"Yeah, yeah. Quite the trip." He wraps his arms around my shoulders, nudges a cold nose against my neck.

I rest back into his chest, breathing, beating. Kiss, soft, hard.

"It's due tomorrow," my lips against his lips, words muffled.

"Uh-oh." Kiss.

"Up all night then." Kiss.

THE THEORY OF LIGHT AT MIDNIGHT · 35

"Yep." Kiss.

"No fooling around?" Nibble my neck.

"Nope." Mouth.

"Hmmm." Arms unwrapped.

"Alas."

"Alas. "

He opens the fridge door." Did you get the chicken?"

"*Oui, oui*. We'll be *cordon-bleu*'d, all tied up."

He kisses the top of my head, somewhere there, where the brain reaches bone, scalp, hair, his lips.

At night we lie quietly, his hand on my hip, the gulps and murmurs of his sleep in my ear, his breath in my hair. Streetlight falls into the room with its dark yellows and blues, straps of shadows across the floor, the bed, curving around our thighs, our arms. He sleeps soundly straight through the night. My whisper inaudible until I sleep and dream and choke awake in the grey. No black. No green. His body turns and snores.

(The darkness was peaceful after the screams stopped. I could hear nothing but my own breath, felt nothing but the damp earth touching my skin, my back and legs pressed into its near-softness, in a corner sitting against the walls, or curled on the floor. Complete black. And my skin. I felt my skin against my skin. Dry arms wrapped around my legs. Warm. Legs pressing against my arms and belly. How the body generates warmth all on its own. I was worried about Mom and Dad, Meg and Max, worried that they would be worried. But mostly I worried about Sparks, if she knew I was alive. Then I would panic and scream, crawl around the black space again, claw at the walls and ceiling gouging the sting of dirt into my eyes, throw myself at the big wood door that had no handle or light, until the peace came again, the darkness. Sometime, after many panics and sleeps, a light went on in the corner and I lost the darkness.)

"What the hell is wrong with you?"

"With me? There is *nothing* wrong with me," Rage grates against my sense, swells into an ugly oblivion. Hatred. "What the hell is wrong with *you*?"

Spring comes late and hot, sweating into the streets and blood. The house we buy, together—signing our names, as if married, as if joined this way, by contract, by brick, by love—is full of neglect and half-tries at repair. All of the walls and most of the floors need to be fixed or replaced, our lives packed in boxes and bags on planks in the damp basement, mysterious now because we've been living out of two suitcases for a month, plunging through the boxes' contents, uncovering useless goods, unable to find the single sweater, the one pair of pants, that have become necessary for a moment.

He drops the hammer and board to the floor and stomps out of the room. The weight of the board arcs and flops in my hand, pulling me off balance on the chair. I tip, slip nimble onto the floor, and drop the thing myself.

The second floor bedroom is a mess, crumbling plaster walls held together with layers of peeling wallpaper, electrical outlets just holes punched in the wall, hardwood floors worn to the last sanding, nail nubs sticking up, planks warping, splinters peeling off and leaving long thin gouges all over the floor. The mouldings are original, though, seven-inch, fluted oak around the floors and ceilings, doors and windows, but for this chunk missing from the east wall. We're trying to match.

I slump into the wide ledge of the bay window. The inner panes are painted shut and we have no idea how to get into them to clean without replacing the whole set. But I love the old windows, the wood and the glass, the shell latches with the tiny tongue slipping in to lock.

Leave him be. He'll smoke a joint and be back.

I slump. Then it will start over again.

We aren't getting anywhere. Fighting for two months, sexless for three. The razors of anger subside, ebb into tears.

Out of the blue, from nowhere it seems, my body develops a will of its own, separate from whatever I want and contrary to our dreams here, at times entirely against it. When he touches me I feel like I am being leeched, can't get rid of the image of worms. I know it isn't him, know it's me, because the image stays, of worms, small squiggling things, thick in my chest.

And I can't sleep.

And I can't eat.

My mind has been slipping. I can't bring myself to care about anything here. None of it feels worthwhile.

He usually comes back by now, or I go down, but he doesn't and I can't.

I sit at the window, poking the edge of a scraper into the hard paint, trying to groove my way down to the original ledge, the wood, without wrecking it irreparably.

(When they got me out, I'd been under
for seven months. The darkness didn't come
back, the peace. Once the light was turned
on, he kept it on, a white bulb in a cage bolted
into a corner, its long orange tail nailed around
the top rim of the cell with small wire hoops
placed in regular intervals to the door, where it
disappeared outside. The darkness didn't come
back to the cell but it must have crept inside
me, into my belly, because I stopped fighting,
stopped expecting anything except what
happened, accepted everything as it came.)

A blast of water hits my cheek. I swing around from the window as a pink water-gun slides across the floor to my feet.

Louis, peeking around the door frame, nozzle pointed at my face.

"Go on. Pick it up. Ya yellow-bellied radical feminist varmint."

He squirts me again.

I slowly wipe a hand across my cheek, my forehead, watch him, fighting the sludge of contempt in my heart, then dive for the gun, sprint to the door as he leaps down the stairs, squirting all the way.

We move through the house, jumping over boxes, piles of lumber, cans of paint, trade pistols for pots and buckets, end in the yard with the hose, soaked to the skin, collapsing in puddles in the wet grass, lie there, catching our breath.

He reaches over, pushes a slap of hair out of my eyes. "I love you, you know."

I curl into his arms, and he wraps me. From inside, the shiver trembles outward into the wet yard. The thing about the girl at the ravine, when the police came, when the ambulance took her away, I thought she was rescued, saved, but now I think she was dead already, by the time we got there, even before they tied her there. She was still breathing. Her body was warm, her pulse steady. She even opened her eyes for a second, just a flutter then closed against the light. But I think now she was already dead. There was an access road that followed the rail, on the south side of the track, a thick bed of grey stone that came from Toronto in the east, stopped at the ravine where the thin rails knifed the sky, then continued again on the west, in another town, one smaller than the city. I heard the crunch of wheels rolling under, then overtaking, the hush-hush of the wind, silencing the birds and frogs above and below us.

A life can stop like this, on either side of a memory. The body carries on, hard evidence of existence, bridges the gap until the wider flow starts up again, but the ground on one side is not the same as the ground on the other side. When they got me out I was the same as any little girl. The worst was over and behind. I slept for a month, took counselling, went back to school in September.

"Should we try that again?"

"No. It's too hot. Let's get cleaned up and go out for dinner."

I breathe a sigh. "Can we afford it?"

"Money is an illusion of the nearly-rich and the nearly-poor. An abstraction that, paradoxically, symbolizes both our highest dreams and our most dismal needs."

A robin hops from branch to fence.

"Can we afford it?"

"No," he shakes his head. "But I have a credit card."

"And debt is an abstraction?"

"No, debt is real," he gets up, pulling me along. "But it's tomorrow."

We crawl through the boxes and bags, searching out a white shirt, a long dress.

If This Is A Woman

I walk along the concrete slab of sidewalk to the narrow path of our house. Step up the wooden steps, my soft feet sounding on the grey wood. Slip my key in the lock.

The door is varnished wood, sunburst window, iron knocker. Inside the hall is wide, bright, square; light coming from the kitchen, dining room, living room.

The house opens up, a generous square of double-brick walls.

From the hall, through the open double doorway, sliding glass doors and a yard over-grown with cedar, bridal wreath, and grass, ragweed and goldenrod gleaming in the early evening sun; grape vines wild and thick along telephone and electrical wires, climbing the fence, the house, the trees.

The biology of memory is acute. In the way things were, decades now, I believed that I was safe. Safe from what I was about to become.

When consciousness splits, the surface turns to the surface while the underside goes under, burrowing deep, scratching out paths and tunnels under the skin, creating currents and flood-paths that pulse and beat with their own intentions.

My mind is breaking.

Every day, in every action and nuance, I am waiting to be found out and thrown out, dragged down for the garbage I had become there.

It's not that I've lied, not that the facts haven't been spoken. It's that facts are only the fragments of truth.

I stand in the hall. My thighs begin a low thump. Desire. Something familiar and unknown, from the other side of the split. Desire flows, echoes, creeps through my limbs. Unwilled, unwanted, a hazy lust creeps awake. A me I don't want to know.

You can build an entire life, create an entire self that fulfills every aspect of what you are, that feels a dream come true, substantial as ground-dirt and autumn, lapping oceans and wind-drift rains; and it can all fall through, from inside.

When I walk into this house, our house, I am filled with such a sense of love and security, such a feeling of home and home-coming, it is unbearable.

I live from the top of my head, the surface of my skin, creating life from ideas rather than dreams.

The breadth of emotion is stunted, not deep, skimming the action of things rather than their substance. I am surprised no one notices, that Louis has not noticed. I am surprised I have passed through.

My deepest emotional response comes from the sister designs of ancient Chinese pottery and Celtic silver. Something in the twist and turn, arc and near-touch that resonates a darkness, a beauty, within me.

My self and identity consist of a series of interlocking ideas, excuses really, a thin platform of beliefs that have no basis in my own experience. I have taken them from television, songs, advertisements. They are cartoons, with the engagement and weight of cartoons.

This is the identity, the self, I live here, with Louis, with my job, my education, our house, our dreams.

Here, with lust sweating heat, belly-churning desire, idea is not enough anymore.

What I don't know is that under the ideas, the cartoon, two bodies interact; two hearts quietly touch, strengthening the substance of existence.

Before Kepler, we were held safe in God's hands and the universe was just a few miles wide. Then he looked, and he saw, and infinity was there, boundless.

Desire. A haze that echoes upward from the centre of biology, surrounds the fragments of identity, becomes thick; weights the idea against the real, and pulls me downward, inward.

Dragged from the surface, the ideas I've lived for shrink into distance. His voice is so clear I think he must be close by, but when I reach out to touch him, when I move my tongue to speak, my hands fail, my voice.

He moves, walks across the room, continues the conversation.

I consider I must have touched something, said something, but the parts don't fit, the response is not of my intent. I remember that we used to love, that we used to exist, last month, last year, but from where I stand now, we do not exist. He is a ghost. I am a ghost.

What becomes real, more substantial and effective than children and marriage, Louis and touch, is this echo.

Light falls into the living room in sheets of gleaming glare. Oak floors yellow and white with reflection. Boxes of nails gleam silver. Stacked drywall glows milky grey, dust-dry in the breath. Cream walls sizzling light on to light. From the back window, damp scent of black earth.

In the yard Louis digs sod from the borders, slicing grass roots with a plunge and a down-kick, hoisting his weight against the handle of the shovel, the blade upturning rich black soil, untouched for years, worm-ridden. The fat pink creatures twist against air and light, fall with the lumps of soil, prod the tips of their bodies into the air, looking for ground. Ants scurry in panic. Dazed slugs curl into tight nubs.

Louis lifts his back from the hips, curls it into the dig, his body braced on one firm leg, lifting and curling with the weight of the action. His leg lifts from the ground, comes down with weight against the blade.

From the upstairs window, in darkness, I watch him move, watch him transform the weed-grown lawn into the beginnings of a garden. I watch his back, the tilt of his head, know the sweat that gathers on his skin, the grit of wiping it away. He works hard, like a man who needs distraction, a man who needs to not know what he does know. From the window I whisper his name, over and over, emptying the sound of meaning.

Some bio-chemistry weights me inward: I stand in my own kitchen, beside my own husband, in my own body and know it is all moving out of reach. My perception of my self and the world tilts away, backward, down.

> (The light stayed on the whole time. It was sitting in its corner in its cage, its orange tail wrapped around the edge of the ceiling, disappearing out the door. Later there were blankets, a mattress, comic books, lingerie in red and black and pink, chocolate bars and Kool-Aid in a green plastic glass.)

Sometimes the mind falls into the body; thoughts refuse to take on the light sharpness of words, and retreat to the weight and fluidity of the muscle and blood from which they came. The body also has its history, its stories and forms, separate from the congruent impressions we cling to.

When a mind is not strong enough to move forward, it falls backward and these stories break open in their own way, cell by cell it seems, at their own time and speed, making their own shape and sense of events. It is a kind of music, brought from the body to the mind, from sensation to sense, with its own necessity.

He digs and digs, metre by metre around the yard, a broad boundary of dirt around a diminishing rectangle of weeds.

With the action of his body, the gesture of his limbs, I am overcome. The blade falls into my chest, the weight of his body against the blade breaks skin, muscle, pushes deeper, to the grate of bone.

There is a *tick-tick-tick*. Louis' watch on the bedside table, forgotten after a hasty morning escape.

My fingers fumble at clothes, moving through skirts and blouses, rejecting their pleats and darts, silk-covered buttons, articulated cuffs. Nylons broken from their packages unfold softly like sheets of skin taken from somewhere, someone, carefully spliced and preserved, strengthened into net. Brown woman, black woman, beige. Seams impressed, or patterns of stars. I am repulsed, frightened; cradle them strung across my hands, forcing myself to roll them onto my feet, up my legs, apologizing for cruelties I don't recall. Acrid sweat from my own skin.

Breasts, weight, placed in harness, held still. Lambs made naked for my sweater, silk worms robbed, cotton cropped of bloom and seed. I cover my skin; slip my feet into spiked cow's skin, shaved, scraped, stretched, heated, made dry. My bag, a swarm of eels gouged and dried.

The edge of Dundas at Jarvis is an odd street, a complicated corner of houses, stores, and warehouses. Near the heart of the city, on the edge of Cabbagetown affluence and near-defunct stores, these few blocks look entirely derelict, thick with traffic most of the day, clogged at rush hour. Waft of fresh rot through stale rot within oil-tinged exhaust fumes. Streets go off in all directions, crossing and turning at odd angles, leading anywhere else, not here.

My feet are on the ground, clicking along, tottering on spiked heels.

Swish, swish my thighs, hem stretching, shaped, loose, shaped, with each step to the bus stop.

As I step onto the bus, the man behind me slips his hand up my skirt, along my hip. When I turn, he apologizes with a leer. I put my token in the box. The driver grabs my hand but pretends he didn't do a thing. Stares ahead, pulls out onto the street. I jerk into the aisle, through a wall of floral perfume. The passengers lean forward, watch me with plain disgust, revulsion. Loathsome thing. They scrape the clothes off my body.

My breath comes short, sharp. I grab my arms around my front, hiding my breasts, my stomach, shuffle to the rear doors and cling the bell again and again, to get off, get away.

Feet hit the pavement, and I trip. Someone comes, leans over to attack while I'm down.

Get away, I yell, and he shirks off.

I pull myself up, duck into the back alley, off the main street, make my way to downtown.

Metamorphosis

At work the women are gathered around the collating desk—a piece of furniture four metres long, just above waist height so that there is no reaching or bending—gathering sets from matched stacks of paper to make new sets to mail out. The paper takes the moisture from their hands, parching skin paper-dry. Old Jim is in the Xerox room, sorting mail and stamps, flirting with whichever secretary is in charge of the day's mailing. Paula gathers sets from the mechanical collator in fours, slipping thin fingers between the steel slats as the machine churns its photographic rhythm, spilling white reams into text. She gathers, bends, piles one atop another criss-cross, carries two-foot piles to the women at the table, where they are sorted and counted and evened out for gathering while she goes back into the mail room, laughing Jim off, humming, then, counter-point to the copier. He slips cookies out of the storage cupboard, chocolate fudge, a pack he held back knowing they disappear so quickly.

The women move in a circle around the table, gathering set after set from each of the twenty or so piles. The paper gleams in the fluorescent light, the shadows of their heads and hands moving across the surfaces, articulate, layered into sets by the different lamps. Earrings and rings clink with movement and their lives unfold through incidental conversations whispering into laughter and silence.

Mary, huddled over the word processor, fidgets with a roll of labels, trying to line up the type, swearing under her breath, damning technology to hell. The edge of a lace sleeve slips onto the cartridge ribbon but she won't notice the black smudge—a wisp of a line, a black down feather on white—until she's on the subway home. Beside her on the floor two boxes of giant yellow envelopes wait to be slapped with labels, slit open, stuffed and sealed. At reception, Jocelyn fills out forty courier slips—same day, over-night, express—sorts them into cities as she goes, pressing hard, moving slow and steady, block letters in blue ink pressed through four carbons.

The women move around the desk, slip off their heels to stocking feet, most loosen top buttons, take off their jackets; a few never do but are comfortable just the same, the predictable Friday afternoon rush, inevitable as a board meeting and last minute revisions and a typo found on page four of a twenty-page document whose fifty copies have been sitting ready for a week and a half; and all the unstapling and tearing out and copying and re-sorting and re-stapling that makes it right again, just in time as long as everyone pitches in.

The men have taken over all the windows, lined the periphery of the office with walls and doors, soft furniture and oak desks. My desk sits on the edge of the inner floor, an island of desks, with the women, facing a break between two offices, a cubby in the wall, too small for an office, too bright to put to storage, so it sits open and empty, shedding some natural yellow light into the blue fluorescent. Tray of African violets on the windowsill, pungent with a fresh watering. I can see the east edge of the Toronto islands between the space of two buildings.

I walk the carpet corridors to my desk, my mind constructing conspiracies around me, petty grievances loaded with hate. Mary brings me coffee.

"Are you okay?"

Must I be?

I nod yes. "Why? What's the matter?"

She scurries off.

On the page my meeting notes discombobulate, sentence disengages from paragraph, word from sentence, thought from word. I try to imagine what a sentence is, know I knew once, but unable, here, to hold the beginning word to the end word, it collapses. I sit with these papers in my hand watching the ink turn to squiggles on the page. At the window, seagulls blade.

"What are you doing?"

I look up. She stares down. The page in my hand is upside down, two fingers at either edge. On the floor papers ripped and scattered.

"It doesn't make sense."

Her face moves, nods, looks at me, the floor. I'm certain she will turn me in.

She hands me a coffee, nudges me back into the chair, then stoops to kneel on the floor, picking up the tiny pieces of torn sheets in her small hands.

"I'll just get these together," she says. "Then I'll drive you home."

She is smiling there, at my feet.

Identity slips out of the socket of the self, rattles loping across the floor. My body bruised skin to bone to gut. Verdant, lusty, flayed, the hollow body swells. I sink into it. Damp, amorphous. It feels like substance. It feels like meaning.

Louis is saying something about banks and mortgages, payments and defaults; he is talking about paint chips and renovations, the sanding of floors, bathtubs built for two, iron beds and nurseries.

Louis is talking; he is asking questions, waiting. He is yelling, grabbing my arms, walking out. Door slam and silence and I am sitting on the floor in the corner of a room half-torn. The naked bulb lights harshly, windows black.

Inside the ground shifts down, and shifts down again, losing substance each time, crumbling then, until my mind is standing, balanced, on a clump of dirt.

What becomes real is the history the body keeps. In the language of biology nothing is forgotten. Intensity is the core measure, so that it appears to be meaning.

Louis slams out of the house, door bouncing in frame, echoing through the rooms. I wait until the vibration subsides, stills, then my body begins to move.

It goes into the bedroom. Ignoring anything distinctly female, all dresses and blouses, it packs jeans, T-shirts, sweaters. Strips itself down and re-dresses in these. It writes a cheque for everything I own, leaving three thousand dollars worth of time to find a job and a place to live. It travels the stairs and the hallway, opens the solid door, hears the lock slip into place and pushes the key through the mail slot, clang of metal on wood. Rat-a-tat clunk.

Sometimes the mind calls to the mind all its parts; an echo across the psyche and you have to follow, letting everything go. I walk only a few blocks but it is enough to disappear. Take the night shift at the coffee shop and find myself living in a strange flat in the bottom back of a converted house on the edge of the Annex, a room and kitchen with a small, wooden porch slanting north into a yard thick with goldenrod and purple thistles.

Daytimes I spend an hour crawling from bed to wash-room and back up into my bed, prop my body flat and curved with pillows, and watch the street, a neighbour-hood of trees and houses and cars, light coming into grey, leaves turning yellow and red and brown, branches scratching the blue sky, clouds threatening snow for weeks before dropping and covering every surface with a thick brilliant cold.

The small round Polish woman, a Mrs. Thompson, who lived in the front of the house, brought me bread and tea and took my cheque to the landlord. A lanky, diseased, grey and white cat found his way though my kitchen window and brought me sparrows and mice.

On this street, the tips of hyacinths spear up through the dirt. Crocuses are already yellow and purple, the air heavy with blooming mud. In the park at the end of the street, between the rink and the playground, the street dogs meet with their owners and romp the grass, yipping and nipping at tails and dirt, the last clumps of black ice in grey melt.

When at first he came, he didn't do anything. He brought comic books and Mars bars and asked me if I was alright. He sat down on the other side of the room and didn't look at me.

What are you going to do?

I don't know, he said.

His hands folded into his hands, twisting.

You know, he said.

At the room I sit by the window and wait for the sun to show the street. I watch because I don't believe in the street, the houses and trees, the neighbourhood.

But it does come, every day, and I have to consider that what I believe is irrelevant.

I have to consider that this irrelevancy may be my only consolation.

I sit, drink tea, pee, and sit.

What is the faculty of body and mind that forces memory to light, wedges darkness from its deep sleep, where it lies, blunting harsh details with numb shadow?

Some days I am fine. I listen to the morning come, birds waking, cars starting, watch people heading off to work, open the windows for air, begin sweeping the corners of the room, dusting behind chairs, humming some tune as it drifts from another yard. Through the wall Oprah will be talking about goodness and hope and I'll get dressed, walk the snow or sun to buy food, picking up a ten kilogram bag of crunchies to exchange for sparrows and mice, believing the worst to be over.

Then, in a week or a month, it starts again, a tightness in body and vision that empties me of colour, scent, and sound. My eyes turn inward, a ragged bit of basement burrows up from my bones, scratching into muscle.

Memory trying to come through, despite me, in the same action of shrapnel making its way through a soldier's body, a piece of life travelling from gut and bone; itching, popping, breaking skin, clanking from a thumbnail onto the kitchen table decades after the explosion.

Senses become dislocated from body; awareness is thrown into a sphere a foot or a yard away. I live within this sphere for weeks, the concrete world flimsy as coloured glass.

For two or three days before memory breaks through, the intensity peaks in a vicious struggle between eruption and resistance.

I wander the rooms for hours holding whatever medication is in the house, lining up the tiny tablets on the kitchen counter, wondering how high the correct fall, how many hours in a garage, how far and deep a swim.

Consciousness struggles against recollection like two severed ends of a broken leg shifting and grating against each other, the then-past, the then-future, rasping and squeaking, pulling my energy into it so I can barely eat, move, sleep. I can barely leave the house.

One would rather die than remember. Yet it comes.

I go stiff from heel to head, arms straight, hands and eyes twisted shut. Sound scrapes out of my throat, bounces across the air. My body hits the wall with a thud, arms against my chest, head knocking back and forward, feet lifting off the ground. He grabs my wrists, arms wrench up and against the wall, then jerk outward and down into the middle of the room. My torso hits the floor with a burn, slides away from his feet then jerks short with his clench. He wrenches down and up, twisting my arm behind me with one hand while he reaches to undo a rope. I twist away, get up on my knees. He grabs my ankle and I slide down again, his body heaving up and down across my clothes, my skin, the air.

Alone on the floor of my room I shudder into blackness and tears. Terror gives way to grief and time comes back, a gap bridged, the months and years slip back into my body leaving the act behind, back there, where it was. I can feel, again, the earth turning, planets circling, the floor, tilting to this sun, held steady by a neutral gravity pulling matter into patterned movement. I'm hungry then, and tired, so eat and sleep, and wake.

Returned to the flow of life, I slip my brown uniform over my jeans and wander to work, taking over the shift with jokes and kindness. Margie stays, puts her feet up on a chair, tells me about her two girls, one finishing high school, the other starting, not knowing whether to take shop or math or follow her sister into college.

"Fall of the dice, eh? Who knows. Thanks, dear." She sips from the fresh cup. "Mmm. Just the way I like it."

I smile as I swab the floor, stacking chairs to one side of the room.

"You're feeling better today, Magda."

I lift the mop into the big metal bucket, slosh it, and lift again to squeeze it damp, waft of musty lemon, pulling the big handle to push the rollers,.

"Yep, as a matter of fact I am."

"It comes and goes, eh? The good and the bad."

I nod, pull the mop onto the floor, watch the smear of scuffs and spills clear as I stroke back and forth.

"They should never have made this floor white."

"Some dark colour."

"Or a bright."

"A pattern."

"Yeah, a pattern would do good."

I squeeze the mop again, do the other half of the room, make myself a tea and chat until her daughter honks from the parking lot. People come in after the movies, then again after the bars close. In the quiet time between four and six, I pull out an exercise book and try to fit the pieces together. People start coming in around then, the big rush, and I generally stay until eleven though my shift ends at nine.

They have found the lives of the missing girls whose limbs were found on the shore. They were sweet girls, impassioned, living the lives of young women everywhere, their lives and dreams held warm in their families' hearts. Everyone is talking about their last days, the whole city wrapped in details too harsh to hear, to bear, to live. I help Annie with the morning rush then scurry to my rooms, thankful for the exhaustion and silence of the night shift.

He was my favourite neighbour, a man who held me when my cat died and helped me bury her in the backyard under the chrysanthemums and roses. He was a man who read me Socrates and expected me to understand, and gave me ten dollars every Saturday while he taught me how to make things grow: In the basement, on the other side of the door, stacks of grow lights over pans of seedlings. Tomatoes. Sweet peas. African Violets. White orchids tinged with red.

At my rooms, Mr. Grey curls up at the kitchen window and I get the crunchies, listen to the lap and crush of his small mouth, the swallow and purr of his throat and body.

It is difficult to place this madness. For twenty years I lived without a thought of him or the basement. I believed in will, and went, I thought, where I wished. But I've fallen here, from inside, and I don't know where to place this madness in the crowd that passes by the window where I sit, on a barstool with a coffee in a corner of Dooney's mid-afternoon on a weekday. The place fills with students and artists and empties and fills again. Painters. Writers. Professors. Waiters and store clerks. Cloud after cloud of fresh coffee brewed, poured, brewed. Rush of cold scentless air with the door open, close, open. I watch a student listening earnestly to a middle-aged man, his hair thinning, his presence puffed with nonchalance as she nods and asks the right questions. And he answers, and answers, filling the air with his expertise. I catch Foucault, Chomsky, Derrida, and look at my hands, chapped skin wrinkled around long fingers, warm around the cup, brown liquid steady on the surface, catching the light, reflecting in miniature the fixtures across the ceiling, and the oblong shadow of the window in daylight.

Where I grew up, on every east wall of every room Jesus hung on a cross nailed to the wall, his plaster or plastic body tiptoe height, dried palm fronds braided and folded, tucked behind the weight of the ornament. His expression, frozen as we passed by, created its own gravity midway up the wall, a gravity that clings to me still, drawing me to the ideas there, of goodness, redemption, forgiveness; elements that are deeply rooted in abstraction but which exist beyond the constraints of intellect.

For a week or two after a seizure of memory I live in a blessed calm. The months of dissociation and fragmentation are eased; the emotion of memory is consoled, but are near enough for me to appreciate the simple acts of breathing, walking, having coffee in a public place, things that were once as easy and familiar as my hands.

I remember my body writhing, the tablets lined up on the counter, the intensity of pain twisting my mind between present and past, and I wonder what this is, where it comes from. What is it that refuses to let go, that drives me to these contortions.

I want to believe it is a goodness, a primal drive to unity. But the destruction of a viable life, the disconnection from time and humanity, the loss of years as I go under, the severity of suffering, does not endorse anything I know of goodness.

Louis, gone for eight years now; me without the ability to think a coherent thought, to function anywhere beyond the most basic level. On the planet where I stand, the ground tilts to a sun that has its own orbit, its own tilting. On the walk home daffodils spear up beside the open blooms of crocuses, their thin heads bowed, a cluster of hooks. A very few are broken open with the first blades of yellow.

I enter the labyrinth of memory and emotion, unable, at first, to distinguish between the present and the past.

The people I meet become only representations of past conflicts. Every man is Mr. Kennedy, every woman a version of myself in some moment of terror or attack.

There are nights here I spend endless sitting on the back step under the eaves, listening to the sounds of night, the silence of sleep. I am blessed in the ability to disappear entirely, skin temperate to air, senses dissolved to scent and leaf.

There is a woman in a room in a house. If you open the door, she may die. If you leave her there, she will die; she may already be dead.

TWO

In philosophy there are no parents,
no mother or father, good or bad.

Of A Common Language

I remember the hands of my mother lifting me out of the crib; the white bars, the spaces in between where I watched them sleep. The curtains illuminated with clusters of roses on a dark yellow weave. For a moment between the weight of my body on the mattress, and the weight of her body against mine, I hung in the air, suspended by my arm pits, my feet and arms dangling as she carried me across the room, through the door, the house opening up room after room.

My body remembers her hands, her breasts, her face, the solid warmth of her body.

There is a theory of love that says that this action, being the first, is the core connection between me and all of humanity.

Still, I am dangling there, one child, one woman, suspended in a small room, in a small house, on a small planet that sees millions pass through. In the suspension, her small hands have strength enough: no more is needed.

For the basement, though, I wonder if even the strength of all humanity is strong enough to hold us. Think Socrates, Lao Tse, space shuttle. Think Pythagoras—a person who heard the harmony of the universe, and was able to translate it into notes and equations. But even so, we would have to fall, the structures of thought and idea giving way to black.

At the bottom of the street here there is a park, a school. Children leave their homes every morning, bags packed with lunches and toys, walk the blocks away from their front doors, passing cars and buses, house after house, filled with strangers.

They run and skip, shout and laugh, their movements passing through my eyes, the sound of their voices muffled by glass and brick. The streets empty by nine.

Here. My cigarettes pile from the pack to the ashtray, crumpled into bent waste, and I follow them there, into ashes, into ceramic, falling under my skin the way divers drop into the sea, spit on the eyepiece then tip backward over the side of the boat, the weight of the tank becoming an anchor into wet black.

What more is a human than this? We are falling backward, under thick black waves, breathing awkwardly through a tube the memory of love.

Lust punches its way out of me, ratcheting with an essential need that needs another person to fulfill. But this oh-so-core need couples open with oh-so-core terror, leaving me trapped between urgencies. An animal consciousness, gone astray, confusing prey and kiss.

Were love so gentle—were I so gentle—love would come, I suspect. But I am burning, desperate. Lust flickers, catches thought, consumes the mind with an orange tongue, skin blistering into charred bone. I sit, quiet, silent, hands folded lightly in my quiescent lap, waiting for it to pass.

It is possible that I am being born again. Or, that I am dying once and for all—for certain this time.

In the ashes, I search for signs of life, evidence of a self that existed before I was broken.

It might be as small as a hand, a child's hand, sticking up from the rain-soaked rubble as if reaching, fingers curled as petals.

It could be as small as a breath, a halo of warmth that clouds the hand-mirror held by the bedside, when even the heart can't be heard.

Endure, then: a memory faint as love.

Childhood. In summer thunderclouds moved in, blackness dusted across the sky, deep at the horizon, rolled in under the blue toward our porch. Mom gathered us up under an old quilt, under square patches of itchy wool, smooth flannel back. In the darkness that she made we lay tangled in breath and limbs, listening to the dull rolls of thunder, waiting for the first splat of rain. There is an arm around an arm around a waist. Our legs folded into each other's knees and hips. Peeking around a flap of the blanket, we watch the day obliterated into a sheet of dusk until the next blade of white bolts down from heaven to the ground, and we squeal, sweating fright into laughter.

Danger, then. And a blanket. Laughter and company, and our psyches melded into each other as certainly as the warmth of our bodies meld; skin touching skin, and does the warmth of he begin at she, or she at he, or do we combine, create something bigger or other, warmer, when we sit so close, when we laugh, screaming together.

In the melting of my mind, I cannot discern from memory if I exist here at all, or if I am only a component part of a crowd, submerged into mass, as sand submerges into shoreline.

If I lock memory into memory, recall the scent of flannel, the taste of Lucky Charms, the sound of rain, is this enough to distinguish an entity?

And, even so—if not, or if so—if I am only a speck of sand on the shoreline, why this consciousness? Why this awareness. Why, in the end, *should* a body remember what it cannot bear?

Childhood. We lived in a brown-brick bungalow beside a laneway that led to the church and the school, a sloped street that led to the park and the lake. Across from the house we played in a field potted with the emptied foundations of houses that had been torn away by Hurricane Hazel. Overgrown walkways around the perimeter led to the square hollows in the ground where the houses were. From stones and branches we would re-make the rooms, play house in a weed-grown kitchen. Entertain with mud pies made from the living room floor, without a thought of the winds and rains that had swept across the continent, making a path of broken houses, highways, farms; dragging people up from the solid ground, taking their feet from where they ran and placing them in the sweeping air. Tossed onto air ledges and funnels that rollicked the atmosphere from the Gulf of Mexico to the Great Lakes over to the Atlantic. Sucking the air from their lungs, bashing them down into the side of a barn. Or placing them, gently, gently, three and a half kilometres down the road, in a field where the quiet grass lay untouched, whispering in the sun, a metre from gouged and broken ground.

Here. At four o'clock the kids start coming back, still bouncing off the sidewalk, flowing up the streets like rivers from a lake. I open the window and feed Mr. Grey.

When I hear them playing in the next-door yards, safe, I go to sleep to wake at ten for my shift.

I don't read newspapers because it breaks my heart, the trial of the missing girls splashing up everywhere, but when customers come for their coffee they bring the news into my fragile mind and I can't help but see.

It takes years to break the case, and the trial lasts for months, details of horror glazing over the summer and fall, settling over the city, stitched into every conversation, every encounter, the unbearable breaks into buses and subways, a paper tucked under the arm, café conversations that tilt away then veer into it again. The words, the details—whispering the courts into pen and paper, formed into print and type, rolling off the presses and photos in thousands—squirming across the airwaves where blank-faced reporters try to hold back tears.

When it is over, when it is gone and the nightmares have subsided—when the culprits have not been torn limb from limb, as the heart believes they should, but are locked away—the current of it drifts through the streets, around buildings, catches momentum and rolls into the fields, the atmosphere, the current of a storm that left three children dead, everyone injured.

The field was razed eventually, a set of apartment buildings plunked into that ground with back-hoes and cranes digging out the earth, planting steel girders, pouring cement two storeys deep, ten storeys high, obliterating any evidence of storms.

The house is still there, though; the street is still there, trees lining the slope of the road to the lake.

And me, my body is here.

Sometimes there is a double reflection in the window, a face behind a face, slightly out of line, so the features distort, eye slipping into eye to form a gouge under the brow, mouth a blur, nose three nostrils wide. The forehead still curves, catching light at the contour.

The rest of me disappears with distance, the pale smudge of my hands an inverted shadow against the black.

In daylight there is no reflection. The street is plain. A roofing truck pulls up to the curb, red ladder attached to the side, and a man steps into the morning. A beautiful man, with copper skin, black hair, long limbs, wearing sweat pants and a wind breaker, steps down from the truck onto the street, possessing his actions the way a swan possesses her wings.

Stepping around the truck, onto the sidewalk, he stretches tall, hands to the sky, then certainly, without hesitation or stutter, he begins to undress.

He is not a young man, though not yet grey. His name is Anderson, or so it says on the side of the truck. He is happy this morning, and well, about to dismantle the worn shingles off a neighbour's roof and, strip by strip, make a new one. He peels his body down to shorts and skin, the warmth of flesh entering my eyes solid, substantial, his strength, flowing from centre, glides through his limbs, muscles flexed and relaxed as he dips, bends to the ground to pull on work clothes.

He hoists the ladder from the truck and over his shoulder. As I watch, my arms twitch with flex, feel the metal weight cut into my arms. I hold my breath as he hauls the ladder and himself out of sight. I walk with him, then, out of sight of the street, my window.

He is smiling, benign. He does not see me. But he is a man, a stranger, and I feel the threat of a blow. I can't move for fear of making a sound, a gesture that might call his attention to me.

My cigarettes sit not an arm's length away, my bladder aches into my belly. Through the morning he passes in and out of sight, carrying bundles of shingles from the back of the truck. I wait, suspended between threat and action, threat and release, thoughts frozen into a glaze, listening to my heartbeat, my breath, in unsteady rhythm.

When he pulls away at lunch, I collapse, move, stunned, breathe deep into the air, pull myself away from the window, the street.

I do not hate men. Nor am I afraid of men. I am afraid of myself.

This was not always so. I remember when my body lifted from the ground, strong with volition. Feet pressed onto the ground, the whole weight of me pushing off, lifting upward to catch the bottom branch, swinging my butt up and around to sit and crouch again for the next swing up that would have my torso wrapped gently around the thinnest leading branch.

Brother and sister climbing up behind. Meg stopping halfway to the top, content to sit at the crook where branches splay into smaller limbs. Max, monkeying up behind me, catching hold of my foot, and trying to pull me down to pull himself up. Boot to the head, almost accidental.

It is not aggression that is violent.

Max surprises me always, everywhere, anytime, coming at me, head lowered like a mad bull, black hair flopping down. Quick one-two flurry of jabs that always stop just in time; the tempo of gentleness at the last moment brushing my arm and belly, feather light. I jump, hit the wall or the coffee table.

Here. Down the street, in the meshed details of distance, a blue square enlarges, heading this way. Mrs. Thompson home from her cleaning job, her blue-flowered work dress loose around her body, carrying a canvas bag of brushes, rags, detergents. Her long hair, grey streaked black, pinned in loops around her head, falls loose in strands around her face. The wind and her walk catch her dress, pulling it around her body, expressing her shape. She is constructed of spheres, her breasts, belly, verdant as pregnancy but full, instead, of years and gestures. There is a glide to her step, a rolling, as a ship on the sea, a blue ship on a blue sea. She is this beautiful. She turns up the walk. I make a small wave but she doesn't see me here sitting in shadow behind the window. Her key slips into the lock, the door squeaks open. Her feet ascend the stairs, heavy, slow, certain. Another body in the house.

(Winging off the monkey bars, the crook of
my legs caught on a pole, the system of life
transversed, pounding in my head, through the
roots of my hair to the sprawled tips, reaching
down, through the swinging air.
Trees tiptoe on branch-tips to hold up the green.
The creek flows backward, upside down.
The sky at my feet.)

At night the grass is cool against the warm ground, damp coming up, and my face goes into it, listening for the low rumble of the train. One ear up, one ear down, until the ground trembles with its passing. Then nightfall, ordinary nightfall, comes sweet and gentle and entire; surrounds me, holding me vast to the ground and pulling me outward as I pull it into me. I lie there, entirely still, composed, taking the night as it takes me, dissolving.

Childhood. The light coming out of the back door falls into the night like an oblong rectangular cube, shimmering transportation, transition; a cubicle, a vestibule of interpenetration, made of light and night but separate from both. When Mom or Dad stand in the doorway their bodies become something else too. The edges of their shapes shimmer and disintegrate, forming and re-forming as they gesture and turn. The smaller parts of their bodies—fingers, hands, faces—disappear against the light. Shadow, then light. Solid, then air. Mom, Dad, then something else.

The imprint of the first experience of pain lies deep within the body of the brain, a physical organ constructed of cells and nerves and blood. It is here, where the body becomes the mind, that tragedy occurs and may inspire transformation.

Mr. Grey pads in from the kitchen, stops at the door before entering the room, checking it out. He jumps on the bed, mews two meows, then curls into the hollow of my belly, the sound and action of his purr resounds through my skin, warmth building into heat.

I lay still feeling the blobbed weight of him leaning into me, then the articulation of his bones, muscles—hip, spine, leg—as he cleans, pink tongue to grey paw. I wait until he sleeps, listen to his breath, watch the rise and fall of his body. Feel the rise and fall at my skin, my blood and muscles responding to the touch with its own flow: implying a thickness, a substance, the presence of muscle and bone, and a system integral to that.

It's a cat here; molded through touch, into heat.

Before. I met Nancy in the schoolyard on a Saturday morning when I was running track. Five laps alone and on the turn of the sixth she was standing, dressed in jeans and jean-jacket, tight-fitted tank top, in the corner, on the train-track side of the storm fence. I finished the sixth lap and walked across the yard, bisecting the circle of the track. Through the hollow steel diamonds of the fence, she told me that Neil loved me. I knew that boys were weak and that I could not say no. She lit two cigarettes off the edge of her mouth, passed one through, invited me to her place on the weekend then turned and walked away along the track. I inhaled deeply, a luxurious harshness. My gym bag lay way across the green football field, a black dot at the finish line.

Across the football field, the white wood crucifix, ten or twelve feet tall, nailed high to the red brick school. Nancy—slouched against the wall, left leg balanced on a heel, rocking loose; hips braced securely aslant on her right leg—already knew how to be bored. Returning under her disinterest, curiosity left back at the rail where we'd climbed over the fence, walking toward her, learning how to saunter, pacing each other slow. By the time we reached her, we'd be cool and easy, all spine-slouch and loose bone leaning into the near shelter of the gym doors. We ride the streetcar from Long Branch to Humber to Neville and back again, paying full adult fare both ways. Pockets crammed. Two private packs of cigarettes. Chocolate bars. Jujubes. SweeTarts. Nancy's hair, thin as whips, scars my face, my eyes, where I sit behind her, armpit pushed to slice by the window edge of the old streetcar, my elbow hanging under my head. Box of thin metal, orange bones clunk-sliding, turning, sliding. All the way from Queen Street to Queen Street.

I choose the yellow dress. Shoulders naked, sharp, glowing under the rows of mirror lights. A triangle of cloth, tied loosely at the back, smooths down from my neck, covers the smooth curves of my breasts, hugs my ribs, my waist, blooms into flat belly, round bum, touches the edge of my hips and lets go, draped loose, bulge of thigh, narrow flare, to the ground.

The triad of mirrors in front and behind crowd with yellow dresses, a woman's face and arms a hundred times.

Nancy says, "It works! It works!"

I move, and the women move, a hundred me's, all yellow.

It is my body draped in thin pliant cotton. In one summer vitality shifts from street hockey and tag, from the steady beat of *height, height, height*; and grows outward, choosing its inches, how and where, shaping itself.

She watches me now, this woman's body within which I am enclosed, watches me as I watch her. I wonder as she wonders, smile as she smiles, shift a hip as she shifts, twirl a flounce from the hem.

"Do you think so?" I ask, knowing, certain, it is true.

He slips up behind me and tucks two blue fives into the band of my pants. I jump a bit, my hands full of soil, tucking seeds into trays of small cups no bigger than eggs, filling them over with more dirt.

"You can take a tray of those home. Put them on the window-sill. Don't let them dry out."

I pick up a teaspoon of hard black seeds, little round pebbles hard as stones. He's shown me how they'll break open, frail green threads pushing up, holding the shell of what they were on their heads like tiny baseball caps, pushing them off as the thread folds open into leaf, vine, flower. Across the work bench, eye-level to the ground, glassy snow clumped and beaded. A trail of water leaks from the corner of the window, following the cracks in the big bricks, a zigzag along straight lines going down, then a ragged swerve to the corner of the table.

"You got a leak, Mr. K."

He comes up behind me, leans forward over my shoulders to press against the loose pane.

"A little," he says. The window rattles under his fingers. "Yes, a little. I'll fix it when we put in the lights for the orchids."

"When are they coming?"

"June. I think. June. I want to start them in summer. Give them a good start in the heat."

    (Boxes of candies behind the glass.
     Rows of books on the shelves.
     Stacks of clothes in racks.
     Paint pots and paper.

Rows of shoes at the bargain place
and a woman at the counter in front to pay.
Mom stands in the small square of the kitchen,
a magician surrounded by plates and steam,
frenetic and sweating, busy with knives.
Dad sleeps in the big brown chair.
(Everything I want is outside.))

Before. At the party on Saturday I was the only dress in a room full of jeans with hems so wide the bottoms neatly covered the toes of the blue-striped white Adidas everyone wore. Nancy had two cases of 45's and Anna brought more. Her parents weren't home. We stayed in the basement, the low ceilings limiting our leaps and twists. Halfway through the evening, between *Rockin' Robin* and *I'll Be There*, Nancy took me into the washroom, gave me jeans and a pop-top. The songs turned to slow dances, cooing. Neil wrapped his shaking arms around me, his body sweating and hard, pushing my newly bared belly against his belt. As we swayed toward the dark corner and kissed, I felt approval, acceptance. Recognition.

> (Flour powder spread across the brown Formica table top. A white tin bin and the plop of a pile of dough. Squish under the wooden rolling pin, flattened to squares, spooned with warm potato and meat, pinched into lumpy triangles. The big pot roiling with pedaha, steaming the winter house with sweat, drip, sweat. Sour cream.)

I walk to the house from school, black asphalt from playground to road to laneway barely interrupted by the white line of sidewalk, a rounded strip of curb.

I wear broad red shoes with rounded toes and thick black laces.

My feet slap against the ground because I have been in my head all day, in my seat, and my body is weary and bored, reluctant to be ignored all day then brought into service.

There are wide shallow puddles along the laneway that reach for each other, touch each other, with heavy rains.

The backyard is grass and mud, wooden steps painted blue, weathered grey. I walk into the house, shuffle off my shoes into the big shoe pile by the kitchen door.

The smell is potatoes and onions.

The touch is the hot plate on my fingertips, the rough rug under my knees and hips.

The taste is warning.

The atmosphere is thick, slow, fluid. Everyone moves slowly. Mom at the stove. Max and Meg spread across the floor, their plates at their elbows, eating.

The noise of the television, heavy, amorphous, washes through the house, ebbs, flows, against my ears, my skin. We watch each other from across the room or don't look at each other.

I eat. Wash up. Change into my old jeans. Say, Bye Mum. Bye.

Light

There's too much sorrow here.

The children keep coming home from school, going back to school, coming home, but still there is too much.

My body is drenched in it, sleepless.

Rain patters the coffee shop windows. My ankle poised out the bottom of the door. Gutter rush and nylons marked in splats, stretching. I run for the green light, milky in the haze of downpour, the beat of rain chasing me across the wide sidewalk. The hard curb floating so far behind, streets filled only with murky rain, sheets that blur the mall entrance across the street. Splash. Street lamps hold their yellow glow so tight, so close, frightened now of the dark. High noon. Broad daylight. Mid-summer and dark. Scuffle down wet cement stairs, careful not to slip. This is the way it will be. Steep stairs and the treacherous angling of bipedal locomotion. The spine, uncomfortably vertical, bows. Shoulders hunched in anticipation, I clutch the railing as if it might be edible, sentient, the last branch.

The lock in the door sticks. Hallway half-lit. Slide the windows open to the horrible rush of sound into muffled space. The curtains whinny in the night breeze.

Summer. Autumn. Another pay-cheque and it's okay, now, to pay the phone bill in full.

Mr. Grey huddles under the bed, eyes glowing in the blank rectangle of space. Tail twitch. Musky house. Shadows drop quickly, scatter, reform. Bath running over and over. Perfume scent all over the floor, crowds out my wet toes. Window still open. Whisper of hoof beat. Scamper and gallop. And, under all that, a scent. Some scent. Of animals, dirt.

Starving so long. Thigh-bones articulated, knobs at the hip swinging, back, forth, back. Curved blades of pelvis, and the cave of my stomach collecting puddles in the quiet bath water, milky with soap dissolved.

I think, How did this start? and my heart shuts down, can't take the tangle backward anymore, threads beaded with sticky clumps of details, knotted, stuck. My eyes close against the night-light lit dark, bright bursts flitting on the inner lid. I just let them flash and subside until I must be sleeping because I think nothing, think nothing.

Only the sense I had to take everything. By that point. Meg on the psych ward. Max yelling racisms only to get my attention and Mom just standing there crying as if the only answer was death. Mine. Hers. Someone's. A refugee down the street wrapped in a sumptuous quilt, neighbours fighting over ownership of the quilt, find her, murdered, quartered. Illegal. Visible.

Later, in my bedroom, wrapped in towels and old socks, sitting in the pink chair with ratted corners, tattered edges. The window, dark as dark, reflects the glow-glimmer orange of my cigarette butt floating amorphous slow arcs from lap to mouth, lap to mouth.

I know my hands are brave as skeletons. Eyes unshifting. Heart pattering a hollow of ribs.

Through the panes of the window, mesh of the screen,
night gentles the grass, wetting the tips of new blades.

I didn't know that the mind could fragment into sections, that parts could break off, float away for decades, return as if *Now*.

He tiptoes down the first stair to the first door, crosses the room with the orchids, pulls something heavy across the floor, and steps down again, onto the dirt that is my dirt. His steps are muffled with softness now, with dirt rather than distance. There is a rustling of plastic if he is carrying bags, then the scrape and clank of the lock, the *tip tip tip* of the key, the release of the latch. My light spills out as the door opens, all over him, into the other room, the outside, where I can't go.

> (Sweated to my woolens, itching, Max throws me
> over on my back, by way of my neck and arm.
> I grab Meg's knees, collapse her into us. Butt-
> first, she topples, head to the carpet, squirming
> to catch Max's waist. The perfect tangle of us
> lunging through the living room, chair to couch
> to carpet, shaking the house with Hank Williams,
> Edith Piaf, Roger Miller. Mighty Mouse and
> Superman fly and land and fly; and there are no
> gardens,
> but flight.)

The basement is damp and hot so when he reaches the bright room, he is blinded by light. I slip back into the corner; face away as he walks in.

"Why do you always turn away?"

He gives me things, sits down across the room and talks. Sometimes he cries. Sometimes he attacks. Heat breaks from the skin, gets trapped in clothes, sweat itches along backs. His body lifts and comes down. There's an energy in the limbs, muscles, the bones that seethes low for decades, and here it is, released, melted and flowing. Sounds flow out of the stomach, the throat. I turn and fold, bowing over, knees bend to kneel, retreat. The energy heaves and heaves, then, after a while, the force loses its push, dissipates, recedes.

He leaves the bright room and my mind walks with him. Moves across the dirt, through the door and room and door. Up the stair, down the hallway, down the street to my house, my door. Stands at the window watching my reflection in the night glass then through to the parking lot, the street, traffic. I lean on the window sill, feel the cold smooth wood, the edge of the glass. The strength of energy has left and a thick sultry darkness swirls in my belly, chokes into my throat, my eyes, covers my mouth, but it has no words and, unanchored, it fades with each breath. Leaning softly forward, my forehead touches the cool dirt and I breathe into calm, imagine my family sitting huddled on the couch, sitting together for a long time, laughing into the television. Sparks comes out from where ever he's been, stretching and yawning, then stretches across the carpet, blinking and staring as if it might be morning.

(The tinsel tree shines bright against the heavy
amber curtains. Wire branches wrapped in
shredded foil. Warm glow of silk balls, autumn
red, midnight blue. A silver star, angel's hair.
Hot spice scent of meat pies.
Cold white milk in clunky plastic glasses.
Bare toes everywhere.
Cat high-stepping across piles of wrapping paper.
And snow. At midnight, it comes.)

Here. Light slants hard across the floor and me, reaches the corner where I sit, huddled, shaking.

Two days, three days, a week.

From the shadows, shapes become articulate. Fingers, a hand. Toes. Disc of a kneecap.

It's a body. I remember.

But changed. Longer, older, chapped.

In the formation of stars, a nebulae can coalesce, cloud into dust into fire, the presence of the correct elements, the force, the power. It happens all the time.

It can rain fishes. Or stones. In 1940 in the Gorky region of Russia it rained money, silver kopeks falling from the sky.

The regular currents of the earth—Gulf Stream, Jet Stream, Alberta Clipper, Colorado Low—shifting every year, meet in the middle of the ocean and collide.

In the laws of heat and cold, warm and cool, they sweep around each other, rising, falling, as they must, until a funnel is formed, an entity of air and power that moves, seemingly, with volition; certainly with integrity. It dances crazy. Across the ocean, it dissipates.

Or gains speed and power, spins and twirls, heads to one of the coasts, onto the continents. Sucks up the contents of a lake, a gravel pit, a bank, twirls away, then drops—fishes, stones, coins—somewhere north or south, east or west, far away from its source.

I wake in the sun. Mom and Dad push me between them, their arms and bodies clamped around me, pushing my head this way and that, grabbing my shoulders. Forward. Back. Forward. Shift. Push. Clamp.

Filthy, I'm filthy. Dirt. Dirt.

My eyeballs ache in my head, rods of light pound into my skull. Police cars, one, two. Ambulance. Pushed down, laid flat, blanket cover in warm spring air. Sun. The sun behind Max, Meg, lined up with neighbours, standing back. Mom is wet, crying. Dad, then, rushing against the crowd. Police jumping on him, pulling him back, jerked arm, twisted body arching. He yells. Shadow. Shadow of a face, Mr. Kennedy broken over, hunched into himself between two uniforms, his wrists hanging limp between his thighs, glint of steel hanging at his wrists.

In January 1997 it rained rain—only rain, but at the edge of zero—downing power lines along a thick strip from Kingston to Montreal. People huddled in their basements for days, weeks, making do with whatever they could find, waiting for emergency crews to fix the damage, make things right again, so they could crawl out, have a bath, cook dinner, go to work.

In the usual course of living we are subjected to shocks that our psyches automatically reject.

Unable to place the experience, it stays outside of our understanding, remains stimulus rather than knowledge, detail rather than concept, a series of images lying at the level of nerves and cells.

Trapped there, unable to reach word and light. Waiting for sense, a context, a reference point from which to enter the familiar world.

A Bridge, Not An End

A year after I got out—no more check-ups, no more counseling, no more wide-eyed looks, no more, no more—I walked home in the crowd of kids, past the church, the green light, down the small lane behind the storefronts that led to our house. If I looked up—and I would not look up, except in startle—all surfaces glossed into planes of light and colour, brittle, un-shattered. Impenetrable.

After. The lights go off at night. I prepare for bed in a near-silent house. Undress. Put on pyjamas. Sometimes it is so black it feels that the night has been peeled onto my eyes, my skin. Sometimes it is grey, or blue, the moon coming in the east window. There is no sound, or cause, or threat.

I slip my feet under the covers, curl around my pillow, and wait for sleep, but my body has changed its composition and rhythms, my chemistry drifts. Inside I am empty, blank, which is a kind of pain.

I lay loose and rigid, present and empty, on the border between here and there, every muscle straining into the black air, pitched. Then, from my mind, a knife comes, slicing down from my throat, up from my groin. Pieces and pieces, my skin breaking open, flowing, emptying into the air, emptying out of my heart.

Then sleep. Sometimes. Sleep.

In the fog of morning, the mood lingers, sluggish in getting ready for school, my awareness pulled inward, away from the external flow but to where I do not know. I am groggy, uncertain. I might have stayed up all night taking drugs and dancing, my mind and body are so sore and tired.

I dress and walk to school, but I have become timid. My skin responds to the cold, quick walk while inside jumbled pieces attempt to find their place. After an hour in my seat, mind focused on the task of spelling or history or arithmetic, immersed in the familiar ordered sounds and smells of the classroom, I re-enter ordinary space, became the other child again, the child without blades.

But I am beginning to know, somewhere inside, that you can lose everything while keeping everything. The house is here, my cat and the laneway, traffic lights and school. My Max and Meg, my Mom and Dad. But everything is emptying out.

You can lose everything, from inside.

You can feel the weight of a hand, all the strength of a body directed into one limb, and transferred to a spot on another body. You stagger, almost topple, regain integrity, attempt to retreat, and there is the weight of a hand again, knocking against an arm or a leg.

In other circumstances it would be a dance or a hockey game, the extent of action, intent, and harm, limited by the rules of play. You can break a man's leg to save his life. Cut off his arm, slice his chest open to the air, all in the act of rescue, of good will.

It is not his body I fear, not his hands.

I begin to divide into sections—heart, mind, home, school, cat, street—each becoming less and less in relation to the others. I experience this as physical dismemberment.

Beneath the skin, the organ that defines, undeniably, an entity; along-side muscle and bone and blood, I am filled with blades.

Although I attempt to reconstruct some of the continuity, make sense of it, I am only able to piece it together like shards of dinosaur bones unearthed in the same field which may or may not be three or ten different animals, two or five different species.

While I struggle to retain my hold on common reality, on the ordinary, reaching out, responding, a weight compels me inward, as if an anchor has been released and let down, and drops slowly inward, creating an ocean as it goes. I struggle and am more or less successful for the first year or two.

I begin to slip over, disintegrating. The day world loses congruity, continuity, sense. Concrete reality begins to recede, I cannot make sense of it anymore. I cannot move through it easily. My fragility becomes more and more palpable. People stop calling. Each morning it is more and more difficult. I can't wake up on time, or can't wake up. Each day I cannot find the reason for school, for friends, for family, for dressing. I force myself. I try to remember, to hold on, but I am losing.

After. In the evening we roll in circles around a ballroom, our feet equipped with leather boots and wheels. Nancy circles with me once but has forgotten my name, skates off, her legs lifting and pushing under the short flare of her red skirt. She glides to the centre, marks the floor with a tap and a tap. Arms arced, she begins to spin— to twirl. When she falls Neil and Roy move quickly, as if one, scooping her upright. She finds her posture and begins again.

I skate around the circle, weighted but weightless, the slightest push or pull of a leg enunciating a swerve or a bob.

Afterwards, at a restaurant, in a car or a living room, I continue to circle and swerve. They are moving as if alive, talking, coming together, moving apart, finding couches, listening to records, candles lit, joints rolled, smoke billowing from their mouths. The rooms fill and darken. Queen Street. Yonge Street. Zanzibar. Hamilton. Windsor.

Here. After another autumn, another winter, Anderson comes back. He is working on the house behind the house, across the yard, across the alley.

He asks, "Can I park here?"

On the stones at the back of the yard, on the other side of the diamond fence, he brings, in the afternoon, a pot of tulips, closed now into slender fists, serrated edges of new-breed petals biting through the smooth green in intestinal frills.

Through the winter I have thrown myself at the floor again and again, have escorted pills to the toilet, razors to the trash, and invited them in again, drawn-out rehearsals for possibilities that will take, in real time, just minutes. Drawn-out over days, weeks.

Always this struggle, this mesmerized return to old actions. Body-puppet moving through the play, strung out, a moment held in suspension, memory. Force against force, heart, mind, body dangling between.

Then the floor. The slam down. Damn-burst and flow.

Yesterday I heard a cello. Each stroke of the bow sliced across my skin, my stomach burning, numb, burning with the shape of sound, the centre of my gut quivering, awake, a solid mass.

After. Sometimes a piece of ourselves breaks off from the centre and starts making its own life. *Slut. Whore. Tramp.*

I climb into the streetcar, the folding doors, the iron steps, put a ticket in the glass box and make my way to the back of the car, my steps uneven, legs wobbling, losing balance as the driver slides the streetcar out of the stop.

For months now my mind slips and stretches into unknown forms. A shift in chemistry, metabolism. Hormones, desire.

Electricity buzzes into the metal from the gliders overhead, connecting us to the network of cables criss-crossing the city with their lumps and stretched lines. Each stop is a screeching breath exhaled, each start a sharp intake of electricity. The vehicle rocks from side to side, floating forward.

I watch as Long Branch disappears, the familiar shops and billboards flipping by, low brick buildings with fat windows. Staccato glimpses of the shining lake. *Becker's, Merrill's.*

Lakeshore Psychiatric Hospital. An orchard there, of apple trees, walled in, forbidden. Heavy green branches, red gleam of fruit, leaning over the wall. Max called it the Funny Farm and I always wanted to go. Laughing apples, I always thought. *New Toronto. Mimico. Park Lawn.*

I'm dressed in my orange suede jacket, painted-on jeans tucked into the tops of my six-inch platform boots. Nancy's red angora sweater curves around my breasts and belly, my back and shoulders, like a soft purring animal. My eyes and lips are painted, lashes stiff and heavy, spiked with coats of blue mascara. My nails, long, shaped, sharp, painted alternately fluorescent green, mustard yellow.

My fingers shiver in my pockets, curled around a small red packet of cigarettes, a silver cylinder lighter with an out-stretched blue-stone eagle.

I get off at the desert-stop before the loop: this long stretch between stops where the storefronts give way to a few low-rise apartments then fields of rubble—dandelion, thistle, chamomile—for a mile or so. I get off at the Princess Motel and walk back, past the long low identical buildings, then walk down past the identical doors. One-A, One-B, Two-A. Six-B.

Childhood. In the middle of the night, in the middle of summer, the lights go on and two hands shake me from sleep. My eyes open as Mom moves away from my bed. Her body is made of curves sharpened with a few lines, like her mother tongue. She leans over to shake Meg awake, pulls the blanket down from her head.

"C'mon now, grab your pillows and get ready to leave."

The big tin suitcase is laid out flat open in the middle of the living room floor, its edges thin as knives but rounded and dull. Max is lying inside, barely fitting, curled up on top of our folded clothes. Meg comes out of the bathroom, startles, and yells,

"You *nimrod*, get out of there. You look like a goddam corpse."

Mom swats her cheek,

"Watch your mouth."

and clamps the suitcase shut, hauls it out to the car. We bring our pillows, a blanket, and sit, in the dark, in the car beside the house, waiting for Dad. We're tugging back and forth on the single blanket and squealing when he rounds the corner, out of the dark, into the light from the bank windows, loping at an angle across the parking lot. With his lunch pail swinging off the end of his arm he looks like one of Max's Meccano robots. We're completely quiet well before he reaches us, shakes a flop of blond hair out of his eyes, puts the key into the ignition and pulls into the laneway, onto the road, the highway. When we get on the 401 HWY, Mom hands him a sandwich and I fall asleep listening to his jaw biting and chewing, not wondering a thing.

When I wake up we're in a different country, sitting in the car in front of a house surrounded by fields already dry and yellow in the summer light.

"*Bonjour, ma petite!*"

"*Bonjour! Bonjour! Comment ça va?*"

"*O!—ceux-ci sont des gros enfants, eh?*"

"*Oui. Oui. Ils ont pousse.*"

There is a maul of hugs. No one speaks sounds I understand.

After. I tap on one door of a motel strip of outside doors. Alan answers, wrapped in a sheet.

There are languages of experience, as well as of cultures. Family is one, and school, and the playground across the street.

I walk in dumb, try and stutter and try again, by the time fluency arrives, it's time to leave, go somewhere else. I walk through the door and sit on the bed.

A body is a vehicle, an instrument, you can lay where ever you wish. That such a dumb thing mutely records every sensation is baffling.

He is a thin hairy man, which surprises me because he comes from Windsor and dances as if he were beautiful. A friend of a friend of somebody who knows somebody. He moves now with clumsy heavy gestures, sidles like a geisha to the other side of the bed with his sheet. I start undressing because I have made this decision, tired of the pretense of innocence, dreams. Undressing to the shell of skin, I step forward.

For a minute—after my clothes, before I slip under the cotton blanket—I'm completely naked in a room with a man. My body is defined by nothing but its own curves, its skin, its own movements as it stands for half-a-minute in whatever daylight creeps in around the curtains. I could be alone. I move, reach for the bed, stretch out under the blanket.

What is it we turn to when we turn to another person; when our hands touch another body, hold someone's hand in our hand, feel the warmth of another person's blood emanating from their limbs?

He barely says a word, climbs on top of me, propping his arms on either side of my head to hold the weight of his torso above me. His skull is heavy and hard beside my face, his hair prickles into my eyes. My arms look thin as stripped twigs against his shoulders that twist now with movement, leverage. The pale white of him flows down, chest, belly, darkness.

If we can come this close without touching; if this is possible, usual, then deception is more subtle, more complex, than I could have imagined. And it is.

There is so much going on under the blankets that I can't see—nudge against nudge, force against force, shapeless without me being able to see or to touch with my hands. Much of it is painful. I try to accommodate and smile when he's done, the full weight of him on me now, his torso heaving into normal breath, my palms resting on his hair, trembling.

The way home is cold. The streetcar doesn't come so I start walking; my shredded hymen grates raw skin against raw skin with every step. Snowflakes flat, big, flutter through the grey sky to the pale ground. Behind me my footsteps leave hard black puddles in the cushion of white. There are days when there is no dawn or dusk, just this barely lightened darkness, soothe of shadow, sustained immanence.

At home, my key in the lock opens into muted darkness softened by the stove light, black disks in the shadow of white.

My breath and feet don't make a sound as I walk down the hall, but the floor creaks and I jump. Bash elbow without a peep. From the hall to the stairs is only six normal steps.

"Good night."

"What did you say?"

"Good night," I pause. "Dad."

"Good night."

Two normal steps. The door opens into stairs, no landing, steep rising into pitch. At the top, in the dark, my arms wave the air, slow, for the feel of the light string. Tug and click and the room lights up in blue, midnight blue.

I can feel them watching me. Mom and Dad, Meg and Max; wanting, I suppose, to be there, to be beside me.

Waiting for me to fall. Waiting, maybe, for a word or tears, or just collapse.

I feel their relief when there is none, when my old self slips out, yaks or snaps as she used to, the tension goes away for awhile, the waiting, the watching. They are reassured. And they stop watching, return to themselves again.

He is in his chair. She is cooking dinner. The kids are in the yard all jump and howl, just like it was, but in miniature, in distance.

I pull my body and my clothes into the bed, curl into the wall, hand stroking the flat wood. The walls whisper, layers of paint pushing away from layers of paint. And the dust between each layer, painted into the wall, wet then hardening, lying there for years, rustling now, pushing away; cracks showing up here and there, creeping from the corners. This low murmur just there below the breathing when everyone is sleeping and I lie there sorting through the different breaths, counting and finding that extra one, the whisper of paint. Listening night after night until I can discern it even in the day time. Constant. After a while I can't get away from it. It becomes a pitch, a wailing. I whisper back, at the bottom of my mind, the low part, which is hardly words, calming, keeping the calm, like a lullaby, and everything stays quiet tonight.

Was I not brave? To live after, I mean. To continue on.

At parties I begin to barter. A body is a type of currency, a thing you can use to get cigarettes and affection.

Sean's been looking at me all night, across the room, around the curve of Janet's flirtations and solicitude. I've been staying put, mostly, though I do laugh at his jokes, nod at his comments, a conversation of gestures across the room. I take the cat into my lap to demonstrate my tenderness and warmth. She lies here willingly, settling her paws under her belly then stretching long, thin, when the purring gets too much for her.

The room is full of smoke and rum, other kids with slack unreadable faces. Sharon rolls fat lumpy spliffs, one after the other, passing them around the edge of the room where we all sit, as far away from the sight of each other as possible, following the square of the room. Pink Floyd pulls out a tight zinging ball of sound, a little Hendrix roughs up the edges, smoothes the insides.

Anthony, sitting on the floor, stretches his arm straight out sideways without looking, touches my knee with the burning spliff. A rush of heat breaks sweat from my skin. I don't flinch. I take it out of his hand—this briefest touch of warmth, a girl-hand on a boy-hand, the tender interlock of fingertips around the damp point of a toke—there's something there and then it's gone. I pass it on, over my shoulder, to Karen, curled up on the arm of the chair, leaning back. She holds it for two. The next one comes by just as she hands off the first.

Across the room Janet whispers in his ear, leans close, puts her hand on his knee as if to steady herself. Her hair falls across his face so he has to lift it up, hold it to her cheek. Soft, it seems to me, gentle the way he does it. She laughs and leans her head against his forehead.

Does a mind heal like a bone?

The cat in my lap flips over, offers me her belly and yawns. Anthony leans so slightly into my leg it could be an accident.

Childhood. The pain in my shoulder is intense. In my soft sleep I have created this hardness, a fracture. Falling shoulder-first from the top bunk toward the sharp corner of the bureau. Waking on the floor. Groping through the darkened house, up stairs, through doorways, down corridors, to shake my parents from sleep.

Across the road-lights' beaming and the droll hum of the car, I curl beside Dad, wincing pain at every acceleration/deceleration. Worry and anger in his hands.

The night is sweet and cool, sharp with the moon. He hooks me across his arms, smokes his damp shapeless cigarettes over my body, my feet dangling across the scoop of his wrist, shoulder twisted away from life.

He carries me and my broken bone across the hospital threshold, dark-dark to light-light. We have come to be healed. A nurse in her little white cap meets us with the scent of powder and clean, taking the cigarette, all-ashes, from his mouth. She leads us away from the toothless night where the swollen stars abandon wishes and fishes and love.

The corridors are wide and dim and smell of nothing but pain. The doctor is male and bald, a terrible light deflects off his skull as he twists my body into a white harness, nudging me into alignment. My body, bound, bucks and stagnates, remembers the womb, the birth canal, where my shoulders lay hunched against my ears, pushed against these heavy walls. Slide down, one shoulder up, one shoulder down, skull collapsed with the need for exit. The glare of lights and all the masks with laughing eyes above. Mom, stoned out of her body, lies there limp as dead, so that my first sight of love is not my mother but these faceless voices, these mouthless eyes, moving over me with deft fingers and stethoscopes. Hours I wait, wrapped pink in tight blankets, having lost my arms, my limbs, my thumb.

When I arrive home, soothed and mended by strangers, I am the broken one, harnessed and mending, my right arm gifted and useless and numb. Dad is my hero, the one who carried me across the night sky, from pain to pain to morning, my eyes sleepy with drugs, stinging with his smoke, the morning sky filled with angels, blue and pink and blue, the sun streaming red like an umbilical scab.

At ten o'clock someone moves and everyone leaves for the club. I stay, pleading curfew. Sean leaves too but comes back minutes later.

I do not know how to do this yet, do not yet appreciate the necessity of subtlety, so, directly, there is a fumbling, a darkness, a fumbling. Within the awkwardness it is only an action, as of learning the long jump or the shot-put. I understand that there was supposed to be more, some drive or fullness, a warmth or desire. Maybe that's what I'm hoping for but my urge is less simple than this.

I can't tell if he senses my desperation as we walk sideways down the hall, kissing, and find the bedroom. I grope through the darkness, unsure where to rest my hands. His hands skitter and float, damp and cold, tug at hemlines and waistbands. Clothes climb up my back, down my belly.

My skin is cool, goose-bumped, where it is exposed. My clothes twist tight with our movements, encircling my knees and wrists.

His hands scrape under these tight twists, between fabric and me, crawling under and in, at my skin, fingertips and knuckles. My hands find his back, the flat plane of his shirt. The double-stitch of his jeans. My hands don't go under: they play on the surface of his clothes. I don't want to touch his skin. My body, uncovered, wriggles to get under him for warmth because the room is cold. It is dark.

His breath in my ear huffs and puffs, moans.

Here. After weeks of watching—his body, his legs, the curve from waist to spine, greetings, laughter—Anderson brings chocolate, tulips, coffee.

For a few weeks, while he stays, I am split open, slowly, with warm hands, kisses, amber-hazel eyes, a glow that begins with his body, coats my skin and seeps down, tissue by tissue, to muscle, blood, bone; and moves there, with the making of marrow, cells, mitosis, the circulation of blood, to the nerves, the spine; a slow melting of stones along the veins, up the spine, into the base brain; terror, frozen there, thaws, slushes, moves.

Something released. I flow.

Emotion is not simple. Held back for decades, it releases in torrents. I have no ways, no moderations.

When my body is left again on the mattress on the floor, cell-memory sizzles into recall with acuity. His hands on my skin, real as real, drawing damp from dry, gently lifting shards from tissue free / out / free. More wet again
and again
until the wet turns to air
then light
and my sense of myself as separate is annihilated with pleasure. I am dispersed.

The opiate-heroin glow of orgasm lasts for two days.

Again and again it happens, so I am walking / not-walking, in the rooms, the street, the coffee shop, dissembled and infused into particulate matter.

The man *Anderson* is subsumed. Taken into the core of biology, he comes in, warms, loosens, dislodges the shards of what was. They break from the skin, loosen from the scar-stuff around them, jiggle loose, dislodge, float, now, in the near vicinity, waiting, travelling slowly through blood to the skin, to the mind.

A kind, a type, of annihilation, which, when it's done— when light coalesces into air, air into ground, ground into me, separate, self, body again; when the formed world returns again, detail by detail; when I am separate again, and the world is back—the light that was there, that was real, that was true, becomes terror.

Somewhere in the balance of things, bliss matches terror and the undoing of one is the undoing of the other. The lock, the key, is the same.

The body, unstopped. In the ways of this darkness my body can leave the basement but the basement cannot leave me.

The man *Anderson*—if he ever existed at all—becomes a new matrix of self.

In the bliss and terror together, sitting side by side, holding hands as if married, wedded under oath, he becomes mother and father, terror and love. Me and Mr.Kennedy.

We are together here, my split selves, my hate and defense, my love and failures.

Anderson, then, this male body, this Other, this lover's body, steps into the room where I lay, walks to where I lay, kneels beside me, then, with the motion of heart and spirit, he reaches into me, his hand dissolving into my hand, torso into torso, mind into mind.

There will be no way of extracting him, no way of denying the memory, no way of slicing it away. He is subsumed, consumed.

In the common illusion of the belief in the integrity of every other person's wholeness, I may become whole, too. May.

The possibility of a Magda. A Magdalene.

I will wait for him, here where the maple shelters the ground from everything but weeds and the glorious impatiens I buy by the flat, dipping their warm cube bodies gently from the thin plastic peel of their containment, soft as babies' arms, these roots grown tangled into dirt squares.

The concrete steps here—and the walkway leading up—are awkward and uneven, the odd one tilting as he steps, each step a different height, treacherous in winter with slip and slide.

His red truck, there by the church, clunky and tall, and his hand here, propped on my knee careless as snapdragon and sweetpea.

I will wait.

One year and two, the decade passing without celebration, my hair grown long, clipped short, grown long.

The grey that creeps in now, slender and unnoticeable in the summer bleaching, in the laughter that springs from my mouth, leaning on the shovel, a parade of dandelions with roots thicker and longer than carrots.

Dandelion.

Ragweed.

Sweet pea.

Neighbour's children ask if I've any tennis balls, any toys, and I pull a tube from the back of the closet, the tennis racket tipping into skis, toss a fluorescent green and orange ball across our yards, toward the net and the hockey sticks and the boys, thin and fat and ordinary, body-full in their pre-adolescence, still wandering in easy affection, warm sunlight swishing unnoticed into dusk.

In the backyard the grass grows high and green in thick waves and welts. The neighbourhood cats nap here on hot days and I've accidentally watered a few who found the low shaded patch under the morning glories the best place to stay.

I will wait, then, for him here. I will for Anderson, without embroidery or baking or theories.

His hand in my lap, on my hip as I wake, glowing orange in the middle of January.

August.

The place where he baked ham with honey and cloves and mustard. Delicate touch at the oven.

Somewhere, now, he turns, begins to speak a name and stops, stops his tongue just in time. His mind. And that would be me—me—insinuating our past into an otherwise seamless life, breathing up from some quiet lake; a loon, bereft of mate and child, who will not howl delirious anymore, will not cackle or fly, but submerge, dive seeming to disappear forever.

Disappear.

The flat breathless beauty of northern lakes, vast—she could be anywhere. Or nowhere. She may have only been an illusion in the first place. Or, maybe she's died down there, grasped quick and terminal by something we can't conceive. Or maybe—the small seamless emergence, unnoticed, of the bird, sleek and black, at the edge of the lake under the shadow of the night pine, she pops up, breathes up, and she's gone.

I will wait for him here, then, on the rickety concrete step, under the maple, my hands clasping coffee cup and cigarette, my back pressed to rusting wrought iron, sun, from late afternoon to dusk, burrowing here, laying it's heat across me and this yard and this house where even the weeds have reason.

He does not come.

A Beautiful Mind

Magda. Magdalene.

The streetcar stop at Thirty-Seventh and Lakeshore has no shelter. I stand beside a green wood bench and a pole painted with a large block of white which is hemmed, top and bottom, with a strip of red. Chunks of snow drift flat and down, vertical from the clouds, slowly. Grey pavement moves into the air, colours the buildings, the winter grass, the grade school across the way into muted tonals, the grey scale; filters up to low clouds.

The near-distance and the far-distance fuse into a solid plane. At its centre a red and yellow capsule appears and expands until it fills the field of vision. I step into the red plane, drop a ticket into a glass box, nod to the images of people—a driver in smoke-blue uniform, a woman with shopping bags, a girl holding herself, looking away—and find a seat. The mile between home and high school passes without depth. Hallways full of loud moving images. D-minus. E-plus. F.

An inner life, of sorts, and the methodical collapse of psychic structures.

There is a place in our minds where time and detail do not exist, beneath every layer of civilization, past the infant learnings of sound, sight, and touch, a universe of pre-conscious biology, where the faculty of awareness is unkind.

I get home on the edge of the eleven-thirty curfew, slink through the house to my room. Alone at night, away from people, my psyche loosens and expands. It is exhausting to be with people, to sit in a room, or to walk on the street with strangers. An awareness too acute for crowds.

Walking on the street, my body prepares for attack. Any stranger, any face, any friend. Senses peaked to the tiniest gestures, scoping intention. They come at me, look right through me, to the street beyond, into the shop windows, and through that too, to somewhere, to something.

They come close, faces blank, barely missing my shoulders as they pass. I am taking up too much space, too nervous to deke in and out, then too tired.

Alone, the frames of other people recede. I close my eyes and breathe and listen to the absence, the silence.

My body stretches across the bed, numb. My skin, inverted, senses inward, an animal in the dark, conscious to movement and threat. I sense forward for a sound, a sight. A taste or a scent. Something that will mark this place, begin to distinguish a shape, one curve of thought from another, the bump of an emotion from the plane of a thought, a dip from a rise. Something.

Over time something does form, a room or a landscape, some kind of place. The walls are rounded and bumpy, distant, constructed of curves and twisting pathways that loop up and over and around.

It is almost black but a dull light glows, a redness. I sense along the curves, my mind sliding along the skin-like surface. Any thought or emotion elicits a vibration, a kind of sound that echoes along the walls, slips from plane to plane, never quite dying, so that the place is never without sound. It becomes a texture of the air, a thickness, a humidity, damp as mud.

This is where the universe expands.

On any given night, in any given moment, stars move away from the centre of their galaxies, reaching into the black, which is also expanding. Light reaches to light, shaping space into troughs of gravity, keeping planets aligned. But the whole thing is expanding outward still, beyond even the vaguest slip of fog that suggests another galaxy again—Andromeda, Centaurus A, NGC 4565, M42—and beyond that? Past the black-black.

What is before the bang?

My body goes here, into the neutrinos of silent existence where a quark is a quark is a quark, and neutrinos leap space without time.

A stone is a body is a stone, and whatever doo-dad that causes me unhinges, leaps away, released from the orbit of sound.

Outside, in common time, my body shirks any human breath, slinks around parents, siblings, friends, shops, school; hunts the house for pills and razors and ropes, some pit or height. The skin burns like blades, peels like slices cut from a roast. I gather pills, medications, small pills tight as larvae, in yellow, white, red. I apologize again and again, then retreat here, slither up the attic stairs again, stretch across the bed, soak the pillow into a cold mess, empty the pills into my throat, cuddle the empty vials into peace, returning chemistry into chemistry.

In the composition of stars, fifty million explosions occur every ten seconds. Any less, and the star goes cold. Any more and the star explodes.

The psyche goes supernova, then, or implodes, becomes vacuum and mystery, sucking light and darkness, both, into nothing.

On the other side of the universe, in the beginning where god lives, a social worker sits, preparing my exit. We are perched on the edge of the couch in quarter-turn toward each other, not touching. Dad sits across the room in his chair, facing the television, a half-turn away from us.

She has wakened me from sleep, has called through the television noise, past Dad, through the fog of sleep to wake me. I've climbed down the stairs.

My body is swollen, my mind snapped as I nod at her encouragement and questions, my face slack, limbs dopey. I'm late.

"Do you want to leave now?" she asks, and my body throws itself up, spasm and jerk and I am running to the toilet, my toes squeezing my stomach into a backward hand pump, gush and splatter, flush of goodbye. I'm sure my muscles have detached from my rib cage, my spine from my hips, my feet from the floor.

She says, "I guess I know the answer."

I nod, dumb, snapped.

She doesn't know the answer.

The house is filled with cigarette smoke and the smell of breakfast cooking an hour old. Smoke and scent, as if each room had already been shuttered, closed down, put away for the summer, a museum special. Furniture covered in sheets, knick-knacks removed or absently forgotten, prepared for a sealed-tight fumigation, then the air removed. All those movies of empty cities, two people left alive, roaming empty streets and malls, going from house to house for canned goods and firewood, clean water. Wearing minks and diamonds in the post-holocaust debris, having given up society, given up searching for people, Mozart blasting from sport stadium speakers, sitting in the VIP lounge with a fifth of Scotch and a cocktail wiener on a toothpick. Loaded gun in the pocket, ready for exit. That's when the others turn up and the story begins.

My body feels bruised; my spirit is dopey. As she talks and smiles and re-arranges plans I realize it is not my story anymore. Not his story anymore. It is hers. I have fallen too deep off the world, barely connected anywhere, so the plan is to pack some of my clothes and to leave my home under her supervision, and let her take me where ever she wants to take me. The idea is to move from my sheets and chairs, my furniture and cats, my Meg and Max, my house and backyard, Mom and Dad, into nothing.

Childhood. The Woolworth's on Lakeshore is a long plate-glass place full of clothes and crayons, dishes and toys. In the far back corner fishes and hamsters dart and twirl in stacks of tanks and cages. Me and Meg twirl on the orange and chrome stools at the snack bar, sharing a coke, our eyes darting to the dessert display; thick triangles of chocolate and lemon covered in whipped cream. Dainty stemmed glass cups with pudding and Jell-o, dabbed and sprinkled with more whipped cream and cinnamon.

"Okay," she says.

"Okay."

We wander to the make-up stalls, tiny bottles and cakes of solid colours, creamy, fluorescent, and dull. We move over the stacks, examining lipsticks and polishes and powders. Meg leaves the store and I wander off to the hamster section.

I walk past the two check-out counters with the grey-haired women in blue tunics, through the heavy swinging door. Cool air hits my face and a hand falls on my shoulder, clamps into my skin.

"Just a minute, you."

I'm caught like a fish. He looks like a giant from down here and hauls me to the back of the store, down a staircase, into a room with a light-bulb swinging over a big wooden desk. He yells and sputters until the police take me away.

He is sitting there.

She is sitting here.

She says, "I guess the answer to that is pretty clear."

In my bleary state I nod to make her feel better, but I know that she doesn't know the answer to this. I can't remember the answer myself at first and I'm watching the room trying to catch up to the plan here, thinking, Something's gone wrong. Something has gone terribly wrong.

Then—through her talking, and my trying to catch up, and his television, and my dopey nodding—oh, oh yes, that's what's gone wrong: I am awake. I woke up.

I am sitting on the couch and I am about to throw up or I have already thrown up, and I'm trying to figure out what's going on.

There's a woman from social services sitting beside me smiling and talking. She has a list, a little black binder with times and dates, a briefcase by her knee. She is chattering and smiling. Dad sits in his chair not looking into the room, the television is talking and the house smells like a bad morning.

"Yes," I nod. "Tomorrow morning."

"Yes, ten o'clock."

"Yes, I'll be ready. I'll be awake."

It's March and the windows and doors have been closed all winter. The house suffocates in a hard winter, with not enough snow and too much sub-zero weather, when you can't go outside for more than five minutes without feeling the pain in your fingers and toes, the numbness moving into your limbs. I'm thinking something's wrong, this is supposed to be over now. They are supposed to have disappeared, all of us, disappeared into a dream. Then simply disappeared. But they are still here and I'm trying to catch up.

She doesn't know what's happened.

He doesn't know what's happened.

We are sitting in the living room.

WHAT TO TAKE

4 prs light socks
2 prs heavy socks
1 pr casual shoes
(1 pr dress shoes)
1 pr warm boots
1 pr mittens or gloves
(1 bathing suit)
6 prs underwear
2 bras
2 prs jeans
3 t-shirts or light tops
3 shirts or light sweaters
2 light sweaters
1 heavy sweater or light
    jacket
1 winter coat
(1 dress or dress pants
    and top)
1 wool hat
1 scarf
Toothbrush and toothpaste
Shampoo
Soap
(All the pills in the medicine
    cabinet)
Memory

1 pr platform sandals (white)
1 pr platform shoes (black)
1 formal-length dress
(yellow)
Make-up (mascara, lipstick,
   eye shadow, nail polish)
4 cats (grey, black, tabby,
   Siamese)
1 bed and dresser
Family dinners
The plum tree at the back of
   the yard
The lilac bush beside the
   back porch
1 brother
1 sister
1 mother
1 father
High school
The laneway beside the
   house
The shimmer of the lake at
   the bottom of the street
The railway tracks and
   school yard
1 leather belt
2 toboggans
1 sled
1 pr ice skates

1 pr roller skates
1 stuffed turtle (lime green)
6 board games (Stock Ticker,
   Hands Down, etc.)
1 library card
The bridal wreath bushes at
   the front steps
Tulips
Sunday evenings
The size of the sky from the
   bedroom window
The feel of the grass in the
   front and back yards
All the pills in the medicine
   cabinet
The swing set
The blue pool
Emotion.
1 red bicycle
Sheets, towels, dishes,
   cutlery
The scent of moth balls in
   the peaked attic
The damp basement
Holidays
Television specials
Christmas
Easter
Birthdays

THREE

We hold each other in existence, without volition.

Wave Rider

There are few places on the earth where the ocean is frozen straight through. Always there is an undercurrent, deep sometimes though it might be. There is a heat that comes from the earth, which has nothing to do with the sun, that warms the ocean floor even where the poles are capped thick and hard with cold. In these warmths, currents move, deep, under, exchanging liquid, over time, even with the far bright surface at the equator. We see only unbreaking ice, relentless white, but, underneath, it moves.

I arrive in her car. Toronto is March and grey. The engine rumbles and jumps with the shift of gears. She is a thin woman, very tall, with puffed hair the colour of dried grass, an autumn red suit. Her small tanned hands flutter from gear stick to steering wheel to radio buttons, her knees bounce lightly from gas to clutch to brake. She is speaking to me, her voice chirruping long sentences softened with chuckles. Clarise is full of spunk and justice, and prone to smiles and laughter.

The road slips away. She maneuvers into the fast lane, around a yellow car, then back in front, speeding, dipping, swerving. Eventually, she slows and speeds on the curve of the off-ramp tipping us into slower streets.

"This is one of the newer homes, she says. Just built last year. There's quite a waiting list to get in." She shifts forward, back, smiles.

"We were lucky. There was a mix-up with two clients and I slipped you in right down the centre."

Her smile is so wide, so white, so full. I nod and grin. Two clients. I wonder if they're dead or alright or if they stayed home. The sound of Clarise's voice undulates against the radio music, dipping under, emerging, submerging to a drone. I watch the windows, the streets passing us by.

I am fourteen, female, able to cook and clean, go to the store, make change, do laundry. I am able to breathe and walk.

My psyche is as wilted and bloated as the green garbage bags in which I have stuffed my clothes, now stashed in her trunk in the dark and cold.

The sediment of yesterday's overdose is in my throat. Everything seems to end here. But it doesn't.

The distance between home and group-home, between the lakeshore and the suburbs, is about eleven miles, the breadth of the city. She drives almost a direct line, straight north.

I am watching asphalt, grey falling into the spin of the road, the whirl and blur of it.

Chunks of memory fall out of the window at every block, drop and bounce, skid under the wheels, skip loppety-lop flappety-flap onto the shoulder.

The road delineates a connection, a path, between who I was, who I am, and who I will become, in the same way as my body delineates this connection. There are many possible routes, choices of roads, side-streets, highways; stop signs, traffic lights, on-ramps; buses, bikes, or cars.

You can walk it on foot, or you might watch the landscape pass, the distance becoming unsurpassable because it is too strange a geography, nothing is known,
there is too much to absorb, too much to walk, because it
is unknown and it is going too fast.

I'm wrapped in the car like a chrysalis, a specimen taken
from the pond, into the field jar, to the aquarium, a little
bit of larvae wound and sleeping. We pass hundreds of
doorsteps and porches, thousands that we don't see. She
takes me to one of them.

> (The pills that float down my throat, sailing
>   on, then drowning in, a tide of water, cup after
>   cup after cup. The opening, the intrusion, the
>   pipeline down, the pathway.)

> (The teenaged hand that reaches out like a
>   toddler's hand; that finds the handle on the door,
>   the clip of the seatbelt, social services.)

> (The door that opens into a house where there are
>   beds and food for strangers.)

> (The universe that opens into a system of these
>   houses, these beds, these kitchens. A maze of
>   connected safe houses where there is, generally,
>   a minimum standard of care.)

I step out of the car. Snow melts in glinting strands across the poured-concrete sidewalk. Grass, uncovered, unburdened from snow, unfolds from the black earth, its winter brown greening in the spring sun.

She opens her trunk. I grab the twisted necks of the bags, the shapeless weight of the clothes I've brought with me, and wait for her to lock up and lead me to the right house.

We stand in a circle of new houses, near the highway. The ground slopes into the small loop of a crescent, making a bowl. The brown wooden houses are distributed evenly around the crescent with big, unfenced, tree-less yards between them.

I understand that we are still in Toronto but this is a different country to me. Large stretches of industrial or retail or residential strips without a lake or park or street-car. The streets all round into crescents, cul-de-sac, not so much dead-ends as loop-de-loops. Everything is new, there is no age, no memory, farm histories plowed under housing developments and malls. Four-lane roadways and cars surround us. The sky is huge and blank in all directions.

A strange congruence, as if the picture of my heart, wiped empty, reached out, sent waves and instructions into the air, to wipe everything blank, and made true in fact what was only true inside.

She leads me to the sidewalk, the correct walkway, the threshold. I have my bags, my orange suede parka, my four-inch platform boots. Gold corduroys. Pink angora sweater. My body walks and carries the bags of my old life from the car onto the curb, the grass, sidewalk and walkway, to this brown door. Standing on the porch, the doorbell has been rung, and I'm waiting, completely emptied out, to enter.

The door opens. My feet, far under me beside the bottom of the bags, toddle along the blue tiled floor. I don't recognize these feet. I have never watched them on television or read about them or heard about them in songs. I can't place them.

I pad across the shining tiled floor, window on every side spilling light and day into the rooms, onto me and my footsteps, my body creeps along from front door, living room, through the dining room to the office.

Clarise walks into the office, stands talking to a man and a woman. They are, *Hello. Hi. I need to talk to you about…*

I stand at the doorway, my fists clutched around the necks of the garbage bags, my clothes. The office is surrounded by windows looking into the room. At the far end of the room three desks face outward, away from the room, toward the crescent and the highway and the sky. Near me a big couch crosses the middle of the room, fat arm chairs on either side, a smaller couch facing to make a square of seats.

"Have a seat. Have a seat."

Different sized counsellors come in, say hi with smiles, and leave. Shift change.

"Are you hungry?"

A teapot on the coffee table. Pale discs of crème cookies.

I fill out forms. He takes one of my bags and leads me up the stairwell, nods to locate the bathroom, walks me into a large room with four beds pointing into the room head to head lined up to the wall, blankets tucked neat, secure, folded down with a ribbon of sheet at the top, flat white pillows lined up. Four pale dressers. Two big closets.

"This is your bed." He places my green bag on the blanket of the near bed. It deflates into a wide thick lump.

"This is your dresser." He slides open two dresser drawers. The wood on the inside is dull, yellow, pale.

"You can use this half of the closet." The door swings open to the empty space. Clean blankets and sheets piled on an overhead shelf. A round rod under the shelf. A clump of wire hangers. A small wire rack for a line-up of shoes.

"Dinner is at five. The other residents should be back from school soon."

His smile cuts the bottom of his round friendly face.

"I'll leave you to unpack."

My mouth has been smiling for an hour now and it's hard to make my muscles release my face. I drag my bag across the room and sit on the bed, rest my hand on the bag he dropped there. The room is very square and clean.

Outside the window, cars move up and down Kipling Avenue. Across Kipling a mowed field then a row of tall trees that clip the view short. There is a bus that leads to a bus that leads to a streetcar that leads to a small brown-brick house at the top of a street near the lake. Waves roll in across the shore, green and brown, translucent then clear, deepening the dry grey sand to wet brown.

Downstairs the counselors are murmuring and laughing. A door opens and closes. A car starts and motors away. My hand is wrapped around the green plastic tied into a knot, the plastic scrunches into folds that spread flat, stretching across the weight and tumble of the clothes curled up inside.

> The ambulance drove up along the access road. A yellow police car. The first man, a black man in orange, got out of the truck. He stepped down and saw me, his eyes, so far away, never left me as he walked toward me, his head shaking *no*, his legs moving him closer where I crouched there on the rails. I didn't realize I was screaming until long after when I heard his voice there, long beside my ear, my body in his arms, his voice there, now, now there now don't look don't look. His long fingers stroking hair away from my face.

My fingers clench deeper into the bag, puncturing the green with a pop. I slide my thumb nail down from the puncture. The bag breaks open, texture and colour popping out of the slit in unidentifiable lumps.

Who are we when we have no home?

I wake in the morning and I know exactly where I am. The sheets are clean. The atmosphere antiseptic, sterilized after each client. The hallway, the door, the office; light spills into this house as if darkness never existed. Betrayed only by the fact that we are all strangers, that none of us would be here if it weren't for darkness.

The kitchen, the smiles, the stairs, the huge uncluttered bedrooms, clean dresser drawers, large closets.

For awhile I am more steady, more with people than away, but my bag of skin and bones carries violence into the safe house, between the clean sheets, under the bars and boxes of soap, around the new chairs and tables of spacious, light-filled houses.

I never mistake the caretakers for guards. I do not feel removed. I do not feel like an inmate. The rules are clear. I am able to sleep.

At breakfast there are five cereals, ten teenagers, toast, tea and juice. The refrigerator and cupboards are full. There is a separate silver refrigerator for giant bags of milk. Pop songs on the radio. A flurry in the kitchen. A long dining table where people sit one by one, and leave, the chairs shifting, the group going from two to four to three to one.

At the bottom of the stairs there is a clipboard with our names and chores on a chart. *Jimmy. Marlene. Suzy. Jan.*

David. Molly. I'll be cleaning the bathroom, doing the laundry, dusting. A gardener cuts the grass. There are crafts, a stereo and a television. There are meals and appointments, group outings to movies and parks, a weekly allowance.

I am adaptable to the point of dumb, a pair of eyes and ears, skin, taking in the environment, the people and sensations, adapting to whatever is brought to me. From this, I suppose, they expect, I must make a life.

Every moment comes and goes. My psyche inflates and drifts up, away from before, away from inside. The flow of sensation and event continues.

I wake in the morning.
I sleep at night.
I wake in the morning.
It is this simple. It is easy.

The March light comes wider every day. I rest in this blue house. It is March and it is April. I'm full of jokes and solicitude, serving plates and milk, washing dishes, doing laundry, participating in house meetings. We create songs and plays and harass the night-staff into new curfews. The other teenagers move out, a bed is emptied then occupied. *Jacob. Annette. Carol.*

Then my time is up.

The next group home allows a longer term, two years instead of two months. It is a large old house near the centre of the city. The streets are smaller; all the houses are old and made of stone; streetcars troll their way along worn out repaired and re-repaired streets full of small cluttered shops. Two roads lead to subways. One road leads to the slaughter yard at Keele. The other leads to the house, a hidden mansion at the top of the hill, at the curve of the road, stone-wall and ivy, the awkward square arm of a new, red-brick wing.

There are houses scattered throughout the city where families do not live.

Houses built for families that have been bought and converted into rooms. Here, people are hired to be kind, to smile and listen, to watch over and take care. The atmosphere is thick with the need to care, and the ever-present inability to care enough.

I move from Albion and Kipling, to St. Clair and Christie, to Roncesvalles and Queen, to Albion and Martin Grove, to Dixon Road and Royal York, to Lakeshore and Islington, to Jarvis and Maitland, to Sherbourne and Gerrard, Spadina and Dupont.

The physical world shifts at every move, becomes something different, all the horizons change, landmarks recede and disappear.

I am able to keep up with the changes, the beds and rooms and rules. In between chores and moving and the introduction of new people and environments, I am left alone.

In the second and fifth houses I have my own room, four white walls rising out of the surface of the ground, thin but with a window that opens and closes into air, cold or wet, hot or dry.

The room is an exhalation to me, an expansion of mind from the walls of the body to the walls of the room.

I draw and write, play music, and rest in silence watching the sky give light to the room, travelling across the walls and floors, giving shadows and light to planes and curves, lighting, brightening, then darkening into quiet night where the yellow of the bedside lamp creates a softness around me that reaches gently into the corners of the room, dispersing the boundaries of light into the infinite dark.

Huddled near the door, the sky is blue or grey, clear; a plane, I know, that stretches wide around the city, the continent, then dips into black, facing Mars, Pluto, the Pleiades.

When blue tips into pink then grey, the black falls over the window. My sight, adjusting, waits for the pinprick silver points, the dots that had been connected into rams and twins and scales, but I cannot make them out, these figures so clear to ancient minds. I think how desperate they must have been, for meaning, to make shapes, stories; from these specks burst random into the black, stray ashes fallen from a cigarette onto a cotton skirt, that move across the window, and disappear with morning.

There is a scrap of blue eyes under red hair; a devious smile lighting up the face of a young woman caught stealing.

Our bodies lining up under trays at breakfast, tilting plates for scoops of potatoes and stew, waddling back to sit at the long table, grey light through tall basement windows gridded in steel mesh.

There's Gaby, there, Gabriella, legs shrivelled, rope burns tattooed on her wrists, her bulky torso, painted lips, round belly, hobbling down the stairs, both crutches under one arm, clutching the rail, coming down three flights of stairs to the basement where the line-up for the payphones on Saturday night reaches up the stairs, blocking her way.

Me there, walking up, weaving between their bodies and hers, never wondering what their lives, what her life, had been, each of us too full with too much to ask.

And the counselors leaning forward in their chairs, always leaning forward, elbows on knees, hands clasped in fingers intertwined, listening, always listening to girls who had no words for what they had lived, where they were or might go.

We live together, eat, watch TV, play cards, see boyfriends, go out and come back, without love or argument, the rules are clear, the distance certain, any misdeed meets penalty with no negotiation, and there isn't a shred of love or violence between us.

If the body is an organism of memory, if consciousness is an organism of conflict and distinction, then in these leavings and arrivals I had become immeasurably less, immeasurably more, than I was.

I consist of a single point of focus—survival in the moment—surrounded by fragmented chaos, embedded in blank darkness.

Survival consists of remaining safe and of following directions. These consist mostly of daily and weekly chores, and semi-annual changes of address.

The world I mature into is a world constructed of new walls—shelter—and cold streets. It is populated by strangers. I am given instructions but no directions, no maps, no context.

If I had been a ship or a cat, I could assume necessity, but I am human, and assume volition, on someone's part. Purpose. Reason.

Consciousness slips from universe to universe without announcement. I sleep, wake, watch TV, slip in and out of fever, do my chores, move along on the subway, without acknowledging the perceptual difference of my interaction with the external environment.

People come and go, strangers mostly; the landscape shifts and changes from bedroom to kitchen, house to roadside, my awareness adjusting subconsciously from independence to subordination, action to compliance, wellness to despair.

I am essentially an animal whose sense of exploration has been cauterized. I believe in society, in humanity, because nothing else has been offered.

The distinction between the external and the internal is abrupt, severe: when my body is alone in a room with a bed and a door, this is inner space. When my body leaves the room, or if someone walks in or calls, that is external space.

The underside of my skin—the veins and fats and lipids that I can't see—is inner space; the over-side of my skin—whatever people can see or the environment can touch—is external.

Outside: The chaos, the ever-shifting landscape, the strangers who move in and out of vision, who come near, speak, recede and disappear.

Inside, the curiously suspended universe of consciousness.

The world segments into small pieces, swollen pockets where people flail in a thick emotional muck.

I am on the bus, my pack snuggled between my hip and the window. Outside, the long drive of strange houses and streets, impenetrable neighbourhoods, communities, store-fronts, and malls. A government office through a glass door, up the stairway, filled with small windowless rooms; a central area, usually dark after hours, cluttered with cubicles and vague mutterings, the slide of desk and filing cabinet drawers, the muffled cries of other clients.

When I stepped into a bus or streetcar, the streets went dark and viscous, we drove through it and I trusted every driver I gave a ticket to. Slip that bit of paper in the box, sigh, walking down the rubber-topped steel to a plastic covered seat, leaning into a window, and the heat of that big engine blowing up along the side-grill, into my pant leg, flushing sweat out of my skin as we rolled along.

The squish, squish of passing houses, neighbourhoods built on thoroughfares, once quiet roads now trafficked. The city turned to mush, the blur of speed making a soft *fuck-you* out of every cozy house, every solid brick, every one- or two-car driveway with cars proudly rust-free.

In the bus we all moved together. I waded at bus stops, subways, treading, waiting for the bus to come, the man in the cop hat and uniform who could not put me in

jail, waiting for him and his street brand of rescue, econ-
omy-sized, who could take a hundred people on one
train, fifty people on a bus, and let each of them off where
they wanted to go.

From the back seat, the city is a fishbowl of lights, only
lights. Darkness passes so fast you might be mistaken,
might have forgotten that you're alone, that there is no
home, and the ice has turned red in your bones, the brain
has stopped, finally stopped, and you can keep moving
enough to lose everything, to not notice, to become a
stranger to the world.

And there's another bus waiting, the Islington 110, guid-
ing its long self above the cars along the highway, pulling up puffing and grunting to swing the doors open
in a wheeze. The slough in the steel steps puddling just
enough for sound.

My body walks up these bus stairs with an empty backpack. I'm sunburnt blonde, and I don't know that there
are places where violence can't reach, limits to what the
mind tells the mind, how much will be allowed before
closing, before refusing to take more harm. I don't know
that the mind lives deep in the mind.

I'll pay my fare, walking to the back while the driver pulls
front, flipping my butt into a straight-backed seat where
thousands have sat and will sit, and we'll be riding along,
in the fold of time, one on top of the other, each within
each, watching the ride go by while we ride, the houses
safe as dreams, the moving faster than breath.

The bus stops and starts without a turn. Snow drips from my boots. The landscape glides easily from neighbour-hoods of small houses to storefronts to houses, I pass streets stretching east and west, *two-lane, two-lane, four-lane,* my body lulled by the starts and stops of the route. My mind takes the world in like this, as a gliding through the eyes and the skin.

Without warning a blade slices into my stomach, carves up to my throat, crosses my chest, easily, then slices back down. In, up, across, down. My mind, relaxed to stupor, sends me this.

There is no blood or pain. Just the other passengers, rocked by the steady warm rumble of the engine, on their own routes.

Sometimes my mother would meet me at the back door, pinning laundry to the line, the wheel squeaking at the top of the pole, as if she knew I had been away.

Sometimes Meg or Max would look up when I came into the room, away from the television or their plate of food, and nod or grimace or smile, as if they knew I'd been away, knew that I'd disappeared and re-materialized, a new and more elaborate game of hide-n-seek.

More often, I would slip off the bottom step of the bus or streetcar as if touching land for the first time in weeks, body wobbly with the unshifting ground, gaining my land-legs while waiting at the light, walking past the Mr. Submarine shop, around the brown bank building, slipping back into the house as if waking from the dream of my life into a reality that had become a dream; not missing a beat, checking the fridge and cupboards for jam and cookies and chocolate milk; the changes in brand-names and favourite groceries indicating missed clues that I had been away, that I was gone.

Other evidence of my absence:

> The re-arrangement of furniture.
> A new dog.
> A new chain-link fence around the backyard.
> A new bathroom in the basement. The planting of a line of scrawny shrubs which became, over the course of my visits, a seven-foot hedge.

Carson is sixteen, plays *Pinball Wizard* like a wheel on a Gibson, dabbles in pyramids and spaceships, and wants to be a teacher. He lives in the north end of the city, but comes to my school for music twice a week. We've been hanging out for weeks, walking and talking. He is a boy, a man. Inside I am wrecked chaos but he doesn't see this. He sees a body, a face, a girl. I suppose he sees a body, a face, a girl. I scamper beside him. He doesn't seem to mind, doesn't know that he is bringing the world to me, assuming, re-creating, speaking the world back into order. A suggestion. A rumour.

We're walking along the edge of the ravine, highway on one side, trees and brush on the other, looking for the dirt path down to the river. He's talking about astral projection, how the spirit can leave the body at night, with awareness, and travel the world. I imagine the night sky crowded with people floating from city to city, colliding in mid-air.

The path down is over-grown with bridal wreath. He pushes them away, holds them back and I take the first step down the steep path. It falls in deep drops. I hold on to roots, stretching and plunging from stone platform to stone platform. He follows, waiting for me to clear each drop before he starts. Halfway down, the air cools and I hear the river. The first bottom clears the trees and bushes and we're standing on top of a two-metre high rock. The river spreads wide and flat, curves away in both directions. I haul my butt over the side of the last cliff, legs hanging, belly flat out on top, feet searching for a toe-hold.

"You okay?"

Our hands interlock, palm to wrist to palm, he lowers me down, his arms bulging hard with my weight. We sit in the sun, our backs against the hot face of the small cliff. He pulls out raisins, apples, and cookies. Between us there is nothing. Our arms and legs brush and touch and stay, and we lapse into silence, the lazy rush of water filling us up. He touches my hand with such timidity, such trepidation, I am about to laugh, holding it back when I realize that this is the way it is supposed to be. This gentleness, the careful approach; each touch a small *hello* and *may I.*

His face is round and pale, brown eyes, lips the shape and curve of a poplar leaf, full and delicate at the same time. He talks about his family, the loss of everything after a car accident. The move from a six bedroom house to an apartment. The way his mother became strong and his father became weak and his brothers didn't notice the change. And he talks about his future, his plans, the way he will be. I nod and smile as his voice rolls into the air, around my head, and down the river.

I've been empty for months now, years, a run away, a keep away, avoiding people, ashamed to be near, flustered to panic when someone asks, How are you?

A life constructs itself as he speaks. A two bedroom apartment, a family, two brothers, parents. A history of loss and a future to build. He speaks and speaks and I listen and begin to construct a girl, a woman, who fits snugly in the curve of his life. His hand lies beside mine. He tosses a stone at the river and places his hand back, closer, his fingers touching mine. I push my hand into his palm, our fingers cup around. The touch is hot, wet, awkward where the emptiness of my palm fits with his palm, curve slipping into curve, lump into hollow, sweat sliding between us. The river light is silver and white, sharp as crystal in the eyes. I lean my head ever so slightly to his shoulder, tilt my chin up, eyes shut, as he tilts down to me. The kiss is made of small pressures, releases, and response. I tilt toward him and his arms come around me, his body encircles mine. I can feel the shape of his life around me, the nuance of personality, his wishes and dreams, and I reach up toward this, shape my gestures and wishes to match, create a self of myself which may be true, or may have been true once, or may become true someday.

We move into each other gently, hand approaching arm, mouth approaching shoulder, hip approaching belly. His body comes so close to mine we can't see each other. We see a plane of skin, a curve. Sound is breath. His taste.

Our bodies are children.

Our hands move along our backs, the soft firm plane, the delicate bump of spine roping upward, down, curved bums, long thighs.

My hands are full of discovery. I have never touched my body with this care and attention, but I discover his body this way, its parts and curves. He holds my belly against his body, searches for buttons and zippers and clasps, but the substance is already exposed. Clothes don't matter.

Under my hands, the full shape of a human body from back to foot to hair.

His mouth on my face.

His hands move over my numb skin. I'm not as concerned with what he touches as with what he has placed in my hands. My hands come alive, become a mind, a consciousness. They are creators. They are tongues. They are a cerebral cortex, a frontal lobe, planting themselves on his skin, wandering this new landscape, a reconnaissance of wordlessness, forming an alphabet of syllables from the sensations of fingertips and palms, the pressures of thighs and torsos.

His body.

Human body.

Body.

Human body.

My body.

My legs wrap around him, pull him into my roundness, my shape, taking his fragility into the strength of my hands. He swoons, falls into himself, secured by me, and keeps falling, forgetting me entirely.

When he wakes from falling his body is still in my hands, but the universe has shifted. We are lying on a bed in a tiny room. There are small sounds from outside, a playground, birds. The afternoon is bright. My hands retract into the numbness of my body, my mind, become undistinguished from the ordinary walls. We talk, sleep, wake. Stay.

On the walk home he places his hand on my shoulder, at the top edge, where the humerus ends and soft muscles surround the delicate connector of the collarbone. He places his hand here, where the world used to be, and his life becomes my skin. My body turns slowly toward him although he does not move me. I have no desire. My body turns to face him, to stand beside him. It seems like an innocent interplay, a harmless one. He kisses me and I have a face again. He touches me and becomes my skin.

I am with him every night until curfew and become his universe. I take his life and wrap myself in it, protected by his history; my left shoulder, dear to his heart, is covered by science fiction—stars and ships, sand and spice and prescience; guitar chords, and incantations from magicians and alchemists, Celtic, German, Egyptian. Layers of pentacles and tarot cards melt and mould, grow slowly down my arm, along my shoulder, my neck and chest. His childhood, his high school days, his neighbourhood. His college dreams. We will have babies, and cars, a house, a pagoda in the back corner of the yard, a pond made of river stones and slate, fat orange fish wintering in the mud.

Then he lets me go. I walk away from him, my skin turning brittle within a few feet, but lasting the length of the walkway, the wave at the group home door, nod to the night staff, shuffle down corridors to my room. My door.

The world ends here. My consciousness releases its hold on this paper thing, his maché of skin. I step out of it as if it were a pod, a small spaceship made for a single person to travel hostile atmospheres. I step out of the shelter of his identity, into the room.

My psyche has discovered a space—a definite inner place—where there is no harm. There are no distinctions here, nothing harsh. It is the old chaos, the original singular universe, but it has been tamed, suspended in place, insulated from outside influence. My life, intact and inert, has traveled with me.

Down the long dormitory hallway, I close the door to my room and step into pure undifferentiated childhood. Mom is there, and Dad, Meg and Max, my teachers and cats, and I am playing. I listen for them on the radio, their words and messages, their promises of love and return, their grief at my absence, their will for me to live.

All night I listen and wait, live here, until sleep.

The next home is a bed and a room and a window tucked at the back of a house in a row of houses in a housing development among housing developments. The bed just fits between the walls, the dresser between the bed and the closet. I'm tucked into the square of it, my green bags wedged under the bed. There is a darkness that comes from inside, from the body torn; that fills the blood, the bones, from the cut. It is a small self that I am, and this darkness is the sea. This bed, soft, floats. Moths beat the window screen, flutter into the room through a gap, dazed, trapped, crazy with light, they find the closet and rest. I go to a new school, my body shaking and hollow; I feel the echo in every step, hear it in the hallways, grateful for the crowd at the bell.

I inhabit my body as a small visitor. My consciousness has become the size of a pin and floats through my body, bumping off a curve, falling, floating in the bloodstream. Conscious-less.

Carson meets me, takes my hand, and I hear a *clink clink* as my fingers collide, look up startled, but he doesn't hear. His hand warms my skin, my hand in his hand in his pocket; I hold on.

Once he asks, What happened? Why are you here? Why are you not home?

My mind slips back, out of his hands. Would he question me?

I smile softly, enraged, say, Nothing. Nothing happened.

He nods, leaving the question alone, but it is too late. It is there again, a rip, betrayed.

At what point are we no longer capable of love?

My bags are packed. I sit in the hallway waiting for the taxi that will take me to my new room. Carson has had a hard time with the break up, calling at all hours, talking and talking until I have to hang up mid-sentence. Then he's there, outside the window, standing, pacing, sitting on the curb across the street. He sends roses, chocolates, a gold bracelet; then notes, small packets of dirt; a dead mouse wrapped in lace, a thin pink ribbon around its thick throat.

One evening he takes a knife from his pocket and begins shredding his clothes. His jacket in tatters, sleeves hanging from the untorn shoulders, shards of his chest gleaming through the ripped cotton. When the yellow police car drifts along the street, he looks up at me *Why? Why?* and starts walking before the car stops. The car slides along behind him, pacing his steps, keeping the edge of his body at the edge of their beam of light, slipping along into the evening.

The Invisible Woman

My new room is brown, on the ground floor of a big old house with a tall window looking into a yard full of maples and pines, lilacs. My bags and boxes are stacked against the back wall, Goodwill mattresses tipped up long ways, dresser askew in the middle of the floor. I sit on the floor beside the window with my back against the wall, the scent of rain splashing across my face and shoulders, wondering where to start. The boxes and bags all look the same, beige or green. I scan the different bulges, trying to discern something I recognize and want. Too many useless clothes already, too many knick-knacks. I haul the record player out of a corner, unwind the plugs and wires. The needle scratches into the groove, hisses and pops. My body swallows the sound, disappears under the base-line, drowns completely in the melody, the interplay, the shape it makes of the air. I move in the heat here, inside a small dark cube full of sound. With two steps I can touch each wall. Standing on the bed, I can touch the ceiling without stretching. The drapes are drawn. The lamp is covered.

My body takes the music direct to the pores, and my bones start zinging, humming, moving. Feet hop and hips sway, circling in and out, in and out. Hands swoop and flutter. I start jumping around the floor. It is close to flying. Sweat pours through me, soaking my clothes, making me itch. The dim lights give over all senses to sound, music pours into me like meaning, comes out of me in wonky hieroglyphs, disappears. It is midnight, one a.m., two a.m. I have disappeared. The world I most want has me in its belly.

On my eighteenth birthday, I wake up.

Sometimes I go to school but there are too many people there and when I come back to my room it is so empty.

I am four years older than I had been, starting on my own feet for the first time. Moved back to the old neighbourhood, not so close to be close, but only one streetcar rather than two bus lines away. The streets curve oddly into each other; roads that are a mile apart at the Lakeshore intersect at the tracks. Many disappear. I get lost often, wandering only a block from the house where I rent a room on the first floor. There is space there but no locks. The landlord, a pedophile pornographer, drives an old BMW he runs on petrol rather than gasoline. My room is the first floor, the main kitchen shared. I smoke late into the night and wait for life to begin.

On Thursday nights I pretend to be a child, in pink tights and black leotard, I stand at the *barre* and feel my muscles do what I want them to do. It is little by little, tight tasks. We begin by standing still. Then we stand straight. The next week we point toes. The week after we step forward, and so on. I feel my muscles lining up to my mind from the floor up, arms arc, hands relax to soft tips, head held at the full length of neck, and I never once think of group homes or Carson or home. I stand balanced and sweating and think that the world is contained here, in my ability to do this, to stand poised and active, still as a beam in a chapel, arced.

When she asks us to move I fall apart. Pulling my jeans over my tights, peeling the slippers off my feet, I go into the cold wet night and try to find my way back to the house, getting lost, wandering, looking for an anchor point, something familiar. In dance, order begins with the body and makes its way inward and outward, to the spirit, to the audience. The fundamental foundation is the placement of the sole of the foot. The fundamental thrust, the belly, correctly placed, at the centre of weight, the entire body can be lifted, suspended, moved into flight, from a small point. From the well-placed foot, the muscles and bones of each limb are tightened and aligned to the centre of body-weight in a posture which is at once rigid and relaxed, exerted and still. From this state of relaxed effort, the body is able to move anywhere in the field of space with strength, grace, and speed.

I get lost every time.

Rooming houses are four walls in an empty house. Sounds are muffled from the other rooms. I have a shelf in the kitchen and in the refrigerator. The telephone in the hallway is beige and lonely with a low-watt bulb under a tiny dark lampshade, its ring weak and rare. The door is heavy unpainted wood, scratched and worn. The doorbell doesn't work. There are six mailboxes. Empty. The porch is warped and broken and damp. The walkway is slanted and cracked. The sidewalks and roads are normal and this makes me uncomfortable. When I walk on them I feel that people must know that I have nowhere to go or stay, so I walk quickly.

The eyes of everyone I meet in the houses are full and empty, loose and rigid, like the big darkness, and I struggle to believe that I must not belong here, that I must be different, that my eyes must be different than their eyes, but in my deepest heart I know we are the same.

We don't have any plans for the future but we meet in the hallway or in the kitchen and sit and talk about something—what do we talk about when there is no future? Rummy, Crazy Eights, Double Solitaire, Backgammon. The babies and lives that we've had. Velvet Hammers, Rum and Coke, Gin and Tonic. Jenny knits and I draw and Dina is expecting soon. Sue moves in for a month, stumbles in late and drunk one night, leaves the next day because she misses Sudbury so desperately. The young guy in the attic is in college from Timmins, smiles but doesn't talk, leaves after two months.

I wake early or late. There is a kettle on the stove. There are cigarettes. There are records and a sketchbook. A few of the bags that I left home with are still with me.

When I walk on the sidewalk I walk quickly.

The grey van rumbles around our bodies, hollow except for these two seats, a rolled tent, and a backpack full of groceries. The engine growls a solid metal square just below the windshield, bringing us through, forward, lighting the blackness around us into black strip and roadside green. Well past midnight we stop to have sex at the side of the road, the emergency lights blinking *red- black- red* with a dull clicking beep.

We reach the park gates at dawn. A friend of a friend of a roommate, who has a van. The weight of the canoe flips into soft still water, sinks with our packs and bodies, glides forward through the thick melt of water. The silence is magnificent, the softness.

My arms meld into the paddle, the dip and free-pulling breath in and out of my torso with an easy strength, silent as muscle. After the third portage we take off our clothes, slather our skin with bug-repellant, and continue.

The theory of relativity suggests that there is no single centre of the universe. Two points create a line; three, a plane. A multiplicity of points creates a ground, and so, the possibility of hope.

I am more worried about running out of cigarettes than food. Living on chocolate bars mostly because when I buy groceries I can't pay my rent, and I have no idea what to cook. What I've taken from high school, besides a long string of D's and E's, is a sketchbook from art class. I draw whatever's around: album covers, magazine ads, my hands. My sense is that it never stops raining, wet summers, wet winters, and that there are leaves on the ground all the time.

It is possible that I don't really exist at this time. My legs are walking, lungs breathing, but the external influences that create a human identity are absent. A few people call or visit sometimes. There's a knock at the door and it's for me. I pull myself out of my bed or sketchbook and answer. Nancy or Neil bustles into the hallway, comes into my small room, bringing their lives with them—their plans and families, school courses, jobs, or vacations, maybe her new sweater or a car he bought—and I bring them into my room. There is a record player and a few sketchbooks, a box of pencils, some photographs, two pillows and a set of sheets, the green garbage bags unpacked again, maybe even thrown out and re-purchased, the contents dispersed around the perimeter of the room, clothes I haven't worn since home carefully folded into a bottom drawer in case I need them again.

He or she brings their life into my room and I'm grateful. With their presence I can assume that I'm alive. I make tea and we talk and laugh, listen to the plans of their life. He would be getting a promotion or planning to move to another job. She'd be trying to get A's to get into university. Buying a new car. Coming back from Bermuda or Acapulco or Hawaii, or leaving.

After they left I'd be washing the cups and Louise from upstairs might come down, or Anita from downstairs would come up, and we'd talk about suicide and the babies we'd lost, maybe an hour, maybe all night, rationing the milk for tea, the cigarettes, re-lighting the longest butts by two a.m.; re-rolling the shortest butts by three. Then we'd go back to our rooms, our records or radios, our rented beds, resolved to check the paper in the morning, resolved to change something.

Once Hilary brought two band mates home and I found myself at the Howard Johnson's at Meadowvale and the 401, crying my eyes out in hotel sheets, unwilling to undress, not because of modesty but shame, my torso mottled with stone-dust scars spoke stories I had forgotten, their whispering script betraying any pretension to love or beauty.

He was the coldest man I'd ever met. There was nothing there.

On Sundays I'd travel home to dinner and come back, unpacking leftovers into the fridge.

School had become too young for me, all the clear bright faces there, waiting to be undone. My straps were loose, broken. I'd come another way. I could not read virgin poetry and hope to understand. I could not enter their sweet lives, the worry of grades and careers, and lived in my room with cigarettes and mice, the pedophile, and the women boarders who tried to be his wife. They found the pictures under his bed.

Without the group homes, the residents and caretakers, the schedules and chores, the regular moves from one place to another; without family or boyfriend or school, it is possible that I didn't exist anymore. Or, maybe the acute severance between inner and outer space was relaxed; that, left alone, my inner space expanded, was expressed in how I lived, where I belonged. I was aware that I existed as a separate body; that I was taken for an adult; that I was alone, an individual within a city. I knew that I was outside, at least on the periphery, that I had been let go.

I suppose these people became my family, and these houses, the rooming houses, the place where I belonged but I struggled against this.

I suppose if I exist anywhere it's in the back sections of the newspapers, the last columns of the classifieds, the lower listings, room for rent $25/wk sh. bth. kit. ph. No pets.

I wake up sometime in the morning. I am in a bed, a room that is explicitly not a home. The things I've brought are dispersed around the room as much as possible as if it were a home. I use a sturdy cardboard box, good for moving, for a bedside table, a scarf for a tablecloth. I wake, have a cigarette while the water boils for tea. Outside the window, trees and grass, and the streets and streetcars that bring people into society. But it is as if I am in a forest deep, naked. While I am inside, I am safe. There is heat and water, a bed, my clothes. When I walk outside there is nowhere to go and too many places to not belong to.

I curl around my sketchbook, blank paper, lead pencil, and listen to songs. Where the front door leads to a porch, steps, the sidewalk, streets; I open a sketchbook. The page is blank, the pencil is dark, I place lead to paper, walk in.

I exist in the graphite that the pressure of my hand scrapes onto paper.

The external world barely exists. My body is a dull breath, walking in air mindless with caution, hurrying back to the room, to the tea, to the sketchbook where humanity and my self can be forgotten and the psyche, wrapped in one old sweater, breathing graphite dust, razored with paper cuts, can imagine contact, connection, a future, from the whisperings of songs played over and over, all day, all night.

For an individual in solitude, what is more real than this?

breath
paper
breath

The bar is crowded with college students drinking and dancing on a small rectangle of a dance floor. Quarters slip into the carnival lit jukebox without a break. They sit at long tables in long dark rooms that stretch through the big old converted house, a few steps, a short hallway, another room. Waitresses slip through the crowd carrying wet round trays loaded with fat, sweating glasses of draft, a pitcher, a pint, plopped onto the table, lifted and passed down the length. Scrunched dollars and small piles of loose change. The semester is just beginning and there's a looseness, an anticipation, after a week of broad ideas and outlines. The heat of summer is still on them, bank accounts full for a few months, thrown in with strangers who are after the same end.

I carry a full tray in each arm, getting the knack, quickly, of crouching to slide the weight onto the edge of the table without the use of hands. They're a rambunctious lot, and I smile like a mother, wait patiently through the jokes and jibes until pockets are searched and the round is paid for.

The first time I see Dana I am crouched beside the edge of a long table. He sits at the other end, quiet, his back against the wall. I look up, our eyes meet and my automatic smile smiles. Waiting at the bar for my trays, I watch him on the dance floor, his long legs, tilting hips, wide shoulders, catching each rhythm, moving with each girl, spinning, swaying. He is laughing, easy to move, careless to touch, indifferent to flirtation. He is the mirror I want to be. Through the evening we are aware of each other across the room, glances commenting on actions.

He waits past closing, through clean up, and we sit across the table, talking the night into morning, over beer, over coffee, over our hands moving between us on the table top, lighting smokes, tapping ashes, tipping cups.

I lock up at four when the security guard comes on his last round, and we wander along Gerrard, Parliament. We walk and walk, buy coffee in paper cups at the all night coffee shop at Dundas and Sherbourne. My people are here. The woman asleep at the table, her face in the spill of her tea; the man growling in the corner, his chin slathered with spit, left hand bleeding, dripping onto the floor. The unkempt smiles of the other patrons, hair tangled in lumps around their eyes, pants falling from their hips. Dana pays for coffee while I gaze at what I will become.

As we leave, the clerk hands out steaming cups to everyone.

"That man," he says, when someone asks. "That man with the girl."

I tilt my eyes to Dana. He has bought a round of coffee, donuts, for everyone.

"My dad," he whispers, nodding at one of the men slumped over a table.

We stroll slowly, sipping sharp hot coffee, wander in a zigzag vaguely south, streets empty, shops closed, street lamps lighting the sticky planes of the pavement, broken glass and vomit, blood and lost shoes.

"Let's sit for awhile." He heads us over to the church steps, a side door arched into a cubby. "We can watch the sun."

He puts his jacket on the ground, sits and spreads his legs wide for me to come.

"Here," he says, his arms opened wide. "Come."

I sit in the shelter of him, leaned back against his chest, huddled in the cup of his belly and legs. He points to the south-east where the first bit of sky pales from black, stars silver and fading from the top of the sky to the ground. The buildings stand soft against the lightening sky, speckled with a few square lights, amber, grey, white.

"We use to come here as kids," he says. "when Dad came home drunk and fighting. I kept a sleeping bag under the back porch. Came here, bundled up the kids, and got them to go back to sleep."

I feel his smile in my hair. "They thought it was a game."

The black disappears, and the grey. Blue seeps into height and a red sun breaks the skyline, buildings dark with shadow. I feel the light movements of his jaw move against my skull, the press of my ear against his head, his arms folded across my chest, and kiss his hand, pull his legs around me, press my body into his chest.

"You cold?"

"No. Not at all."

There is an ease and comfort where our bodies touch, an absence of threat or defense, which is new to me. Love, I think, and the word surprises me. The roundness of it works its way down through sleepy layers, almost touches something before it strikes against a coldness, an absence, and I am afraid.

"You're sure you're not cold?" he catches the shiver in me. I shake my head, exhaling the caught breath. The warmth of the two of us reflects and expands until even my toes are not cold, my hands, the tip of my nose. The first light throws long shadows across the church-yard, street lamps and fence posts spiked across the green morning grass. We empty our cups, wander down to the pier, the ferry docks where we take the boat across the harbour, fall asleep in the sand on Hanlan's Point, waves coming into shore, ants creeping across our skin.

I will phone him in the evening and we will talk and he will come to my porch at three in the morning, tap on the black night-glass of my window until I wake and tap back. I will turn the lock in the door slowly, quietly, waiting for the whisper of the click, not waking the other rooms; open the door, my pale green robe moving with me like a second skin, clinging from shoulder to breast, belly to hip to ankle, and he will follow me, stepping softly in the quiet house, into my room, undressing. We will whisper under the blankets until he falls asleep. I will curl into the warmth of him, lie awake listening to his sounds until the first sparrow chirps and the room turns grey with light. When he wakes, we kiss and make love and it is a slow thing, a gesture that moves from belly and belly, skin and skin, as if it were always there and only needed a glance, a nod, the vague intention of a touch, to become touch. It is as easy as waking. There is a glow from my groin, a heat thumping with my heart, my mouth, my hands, that meets his mouth, his hands, a warmth that becomes us, body to body, that comes and fills and encases the days, the nights, away from cold-ness, strangeness, unkind things. We move into it, sink down, under, travelling into darkness, softness, as if into a wide deep sleep, soft dream, sinking under the flow of blood from the heart, through muscle, unnoticed, unknown, beat after beat from birth to here, where we lie, he lies, I lie beside we, and the nature of time opens another pocket, another loophole, through which we can slip without trying, without hiding, without saying exactly what we mean, trying to explain, articulate, what is only dark and dream and we, lying so close, so near, unfeared.

When he peaks, he breaks, cries, crashes in my arms. I hold him until it stops, wondering why this grief, from where. When he comes back, I move to make tea. He says, No. Stay. His head on my breast, his hand on my heart, legs curling up around my hip, my waist.

In the day we are single. He goes to his classes, I go to my job, we date other people, hang out, lives separate in the hierarchy of class, our connection unspoken. Secret, I think, because it is rare, too rare, too good, to expose to crowds. After his classes he crowds in with his friends and I am the waitress. If we meet at parties, we smile and kiss like old friends then spend our evenings separately, talking, dancing, with whomever is around, leave at separate times, make our way to separate places. It is a way of being and not being, of risking and not risking, of loving and not loving. It is a way of appearing strong when I'm not strong because the truth is my body is filled with the need of him, the question, all the time.

I weather three of his public girlfriends, countless one night stands, before Diane comes with the crowd.

"Waitress!" I hear. "Is she deaf, do you think?"

"Waitress!" She stands as if on a podium. "Bring me another theory!"

Laughter.

I make my way to the table. She sits beside him, an arm propped on his shoulder. He almost nods, doesn't speak. She chatters. Minister's daughter.

"What'll it be, kids?"

She laughs, turns to him, and I disappear. Twice.

Once more he comes. We are careful to hold our bodies as we've always held our bodies, then pull the blanket more snug, yawn in a breath or two, go limp then, as if sleeping, until he lets go of his breath and sleeps. I think of Carson, standing on the street, the long white florist's box bent under his arm, rose-heads sticking out the top every which way, their redness black under the street-lamp, against the white twisted cardboard.

When he wakes I pretend I'm sleeping and he pretends he doesn't know. He dresses, kisses the top of my head and leaves.

I walk down the stairs in my old blue jeans, mud-stained from the work I'd done. I have made a room, he says, a special room. For the orchids. Here will be only orchids.

Come see.

I bend under the small doorway dug out of the wall. Smell the damp earth. It's dark, Mr. Kennedy. Where's the light? At the back. His voice sounds strange, strangled, low. I turn. Are you okay, Mr.Kennedy? My body thumps into the room, onto dirt. The door slams to the clank of a padlock.

The landlord took me skiing, with one of his wives. Gave me some tips, set me at the top of a hill, and watched me fall into the cushion of white, my elastic limbs bending into painful ideas. I hauled myself up, pointed my body in the right direction (away from the red fire fence), glided and fell again. It was an exhilarating day, the drive home sleepy as hot chocolate.

Once he gave me a bracelet, a gold bracelet, and I didn't understand. I clipped it on my wrist, held it to the light, and thought what a good-hearted selfless man he was.

My body is long and curved. The bones show sharp under my skin. My skin is smooth, beige in winter, tawny in summer. When I stand naked after a bath, skin stretched from toes to knees, hips to breasts, arms and shoulders sheathed, skull encased by skin; I can feel my bones, the curved rods of them placed tip to tip, the delicate arc of their length, the intricate shapes of their ends, constructed into a foundation, a solid frame of existence. A thought, an awareness, inside a pile of skin and bones.

The towel is rough and damp against my wet skin, the bathroom mirror clouded and streaked. My hair squeaks with tangles, a mass of clumped webs with no function but to grow.

I am clean.

I have found my place, at the Royal Bank of Canada, one of the largest banks in the country, with thousands of branches dotted across the country, Victoria to Winnipeg to Charlottetown. I feel connected to something larger than myself, a broad entity full of human activity. It is an institution, an organization, of human activity. It has presence in the world, in society. It is a platform, a plateau, solid.

I've left something behind and step into a green cotton skirt, a loose blue sweater, a pair of sweet tan pumps whose heels have worn through once and been replaced, and worn down again. My skirt reaches to the knee, my sweater to the throat. There is no sense of the sexual about me, no sense of the girl that I was. Still my body is long and curved, and the sharpness of my bones shows through the skin, articulates my wrists and ankles, my chin and face in a way that might solicit the wrong response.

My face is naked throughout the day and night, into the weeks and months since I recognized that no one would feed me, scoured the paper for skill-less jobs, learned how to find an address, a building, a suite number, among the huge buildings along the subway line downtown. I emerge from the train, pushed along in the crowd, moving up escalators, through turnstiles, through tiled corridors and tight stairwells into daylight and a plane of concrete that skirts each building, stretches into all corners, and continues on, north, south, uptown, downtown.

The black tower exists as sheer height breaking out of the sidewalk with abrupt surprise, as if it also cannot tell the reason for its being, its purpose, but appeared here one day, scorching black against blue, beautiful and vaguely humiliated, embarrassed to take up space, grateful to be entered, to be useful. The crowd is as anonymous as my body, pushing along to our respective banks of elevators, watching our lives go up, up with the lit and extinguished numbers, coffee cups hot in our hands.

I have found my place. It is on the bottom ground of ordinary. I am the Internal Messenger for the three floors of the south building, moving from the heavy bags and cubbyholes of the mailroom, through each office of every floor, the folders in my cart tucked thick with correspondence, our names ordered by geography and alphabet, our geography ordered by function, our function ordered too, by value, but by what standard I am not aware. There is a peace and order in the daily routine, faces and rooms that become familiar to names, deliveries which acquire a likeness to the individual, a distinction that identifies the mail to the person to the room. I move everywhere twice a day, breaking for lunch and an hour on each side to file magazines and periodicals, legal binders where whole sections are tossed to accommodate a new paragraph; to maintain continuity, flow; to avoid the appearance of mistake or after-thought.

I am careful to walk without swaying, to move from the centre of my body and to stand tall. I am careful, also, to smile and say hello to everyone with equal welcome. At lunch I buy a milk and eat my sandwich on one of the stone benches in the courtyard, holding my knees pressed tight, my back straight, my hands lightly in my lap. There is no sky here, downtown, except straight up. We are always in shadow, a constant buzzing of movement, rushing across the courtyard in diagonals, sitting for a moment to eat or smoke or talk, then buzzing up again, the appointment to begin, the lunch break to end, the re-entry into the function and purpose of our work. I am almost happy here, immersed in the clean lines of our clothes and the buildings and the routine, living inside the stable grid of commerce. It is a simple place, with a clear focus, clear boundaries. Millions are gathered and lost and gathered up again, and not a single body is injured.

I didn't know that the mind can shut down and the body could continue breathing, that a body can walk away from a mind. At night the balcony stretches wide with a dark sky and the city is laid out across the ground, lumpy with architecture, busy with lights. Buildings cluster in blocks that are cut straight down by roads where headlights and taillights gleam on the tips of moving shadows, a stream

204 · ELIZABETH UKRAINETZ

of white moving against a stream of red, crossing, stopping, crossing. If I could reach down, scoop handfuls of it up, slather it on my skin, push it deep and let it dry, I would know something then. I could get back in. I watch it most of the night, then step back.

My room is empty except for a mattress on the floor, the clothes I need for work, a bowl, a cup, a pot. The walls are blue. Every second Thursday there is a deposit in my bank account. Currency. This week I will buy a skirt, a frying pan, and three pencils. Two weeks from now I will buy a bath towel and a glass. These are human things.

The skirt is pale grey, cotton, with a silver-grey lining. It is cut to follow the shape of my hips, thighs, and bum; with a zipper at middle back and two grey buttons on a tab that reaches across the slit of the zipper. The back seam breaks three inches up from the hem to give room for walking; running is ridiculous. The frying pan is ten inches across, good for a single egg or a pound of hamburger. It is cast iron, dull grey now, but it will turn a pure deep black, cured at a long low heat in the oven, covered with oil. It will last forever. The pencils are 4B, a very soft lead that gives itself up easily as it pushes into the paper, leaving trails of grey smudge from ghost to shadow to line. I will be happy with this. With a third skirt I will breathe easier on the subway and at work. With the frying pan I will buy eggs and meat. With the pencils I will sit the nights, not watching the city.

A bath towel is a wonderful thing. To wrap the body dry as if it were a child.

Drinking glasses are not necessary inasmuch as cups do the same thing. It is a luxury.

The ground that comes under you when you are starting yourself over is very thin and bare. There is not much to a life, to a body, to start with; not much from which to begin. In fact, there is nothing, but something can be made up. I had heard about things when I was growing up, things that existed—education, art, marriage—I think if I am very careful and stay very focused, I will find my way there. I know it will take some time. I know the only way from here to there, from nothing to something, is me. The idea that I am wrong, completely wrong, does not occur in the context of my experience. Too jumbled to breathe, I do not have context. I do not have memory.

My hands sweat against the rail. Tomorrow I will go shopping and, in a year or two—or three? Who knows—I will have something, I will be something, and I can begin to live with people again. No one will know, rumours will be gone, and I will be able to begin as if I had existed the entire time. This is the value of strangers.

FOUR

To love what is beautiful requires nothing.

The Art Of Maintenance

There is a woman in a room in a house. If you open the door, she may die. If you leave her there, she will die. She may already be dead.

When I met Louis he was very kind. He met me every day after work for months. I would try leaving by different doors, at different times, hiding behind a newstand before hailing a cab and jumping in. But he persisted. He'd find me, be at the door when I arrived home, or the telephone ringing and ringing into the night, me sitting quiet in the dark crawling to the cupboard to eat dry cereal, leaning against the wall on the floor. I understood that I could not say no, and also that I must say no. When he found my office he showed up in the lobby every day. Everybody liked him. Even my boss came out for a chat, as a matter of routine, eventually bringing coffee for them both. They'd talk computers, philosophy, sports, and a year later he was hired. He's a fascinating man. Did you know, for instance, that if the sun went out we wouldn't see it for eight minutes? It is that far away, that many light years distant. And, if it did go out, we *would* see it because gravity is slower than light and would continue its pull a few minutes longer than darkness. We would see the darkness, then, held to the surface by the earth's pull, drift, all of us, into chill black space.

I creep to the coffee shop at midnight, work my shift, slip home mid-morning into grey sheets that do not care for sleep. The heart beats and beats, and I smoke. Somewhere, in and out, the psyche beats too, ticking away between dream and day. Mail slips through the slot with a heavy clang. Once, the telephone rings a non-mechanical trill, going on and off and on.

I have a bowl, a cup, a pot.

Nine years have passed without me, the earth spinning her days.

I remember my mother's hands, holding me there, dangling between the mattress and her breast. And my father, too. As soon as my back was strong enough to stand, he'd cup my feet in his palm, holding my waist until I caught the rigidity of straight. Standing there in the palm of his hand, he'd lift me up, up; my mom and aunts squealing, reaching up for my fall, my face delirious happy as I rose past his shoulder, above his head, the strength of his arm fused to the soles of my feet, watching the world grow high. Then swoop, swoop, my body arced into the flight of his arms, down.

After I left Louis, I wept and wept. My heart broke open, flooded out and I had no idea how to ride it. So that when I left, I believed I had disappeared. The streets were never so naked, so hard. I had never felt so exposed as when I walked down that street with my small bag and a thousand dollars, walking numb, not numb anymore, but bruised through, thoughts obliterated with pain, familiar streets alien. I could not decipher street signs, traffic lights, gestures. I walked, slept by the railway ties; rocking myself there, holding myself between the railroad, the stones, and the nubs of wood slats sticking out, biting wood into stone.

In the morning I had wet myself and the sky had wet me too. My bag was soaked. A dog sniffed my face, peed on my knees, warmth seeping down, scent seeping up; then it wandered down the rail, into the grey distance where the sky was just brightening to blue.

The sky seeped into my eyes, cut short with the grey city. I watched the sun the whole day, my neck shifting the tilt of my head to the apex, following the penumbra until my eyes were numb and I looked straight into the core of it. Sun spots roiling black on red. The yellow disk. Then blackness. Blackness. I could tell night by cold, day by warmth. As my body thawed, the pain came, and my thoughts reformed. I thought, This is love.

When Mrs. Thompson found me I could only see out of the edges of my eyes. I heard the shuffling of stones, rhythmic clunk and spill. She stooped down in front of me, two knees, two shoulders, blackness in between.

"Child," she said. "Child."

"I'm not—"

"What are you doing?"

"I'm not a child."

"No. No. But what are you doing here?"

Her hands on her knees squatting. My head shaking back and forth trying to fit her in.

"You shouldn't be here."

The flood breaks and I cry.

"I can't. I can't."

Collapsing into her arms, warmth, rocking. I can't stop crying, she pulls me to my feet, leads me down the slope, the street.

When they got me out of the basement Mom put me straight into the tub. She peeled my clothes from my arms and legs, tossing the slimy things at Dad.

"Burn them," she said.

"But the police—"

"Burn them."

And he did. Right there and then, he built a fire in the yard and let the ashes spark up, riding the smoke and wind to the sky. I stayed in the tub, Mom filling and re-filling the heat and suds for hours, until my skin wrinkled ancient, translucent, watching through the window the sparks rise in smoke.

Mrs. Thompson brought me to these rooms, a room and a kitchen with a back porch. I disappeared, my body dis-solving into black, psyche falling endless down, crying for days, until, exhausted, I slept.

When I woke it was night. I was on a carpet with a blan-ket and a pillow, a small lamp burning low in the cor-ner. I felt purely calm, emptied of all necessity except the weight of injury. That is where the room turned to grey, then light, and I realized I could see again, the centre of things, the whole of the room. When I got up in the pale light, Mr. Grey was parked outside the window, stretch-ing up when he saw me, as if he'd been waiting for me all along. I opened the window, let him in with the air, breeze, sky. My hand under his chin pulled me back.

Basement flashbacks continue to come hard and heavy, creeping up on me. There's no flash about them: they last months, sometimes more than a year. Even though I know their ways so intimately, they surprise me still. My mind has to step outside to look in, to see it coming. Dishes piling up in the sink. Hair unwashed. Images of knives pursuing until finally I click it in: here comes another one. There's little to do but ride it out, keeping the place free of pills and razors, taking care of the impulse as I would a wounded dog.

They come, swell, break. Eventually they pass. But years disappear under it.

Sometimes, in the morning, when I'm walking home from work, I follow the few blocks back. In the steps that I take the streets, the lights, the shops remember who I was and I can feel the woman I almost became slipping over me, a light armor, an encasement. Remember the jokes, the plans, the high-heeled pumps. Almost, I remember touch, his touch. The way he woke in the morning, or slept at night; the way he turned from the sink when he was washing dishes; or lifted a towel from the bathroom floor. Little no-moment things that barely count as memory but come now, warm, full of image and time, a life held in these moments.

As I approach our house I become frightened. What was it. What was it there that scared me so?

Two years ago, or three, I saw them together. Sarah and Louis. Holding hands as they walked, fairly skipped along. She had grown her hair to my length, wore my old sweater, the blue with the silver shell buttons thin as satin. They looked happy and I remembered myself this way, Louis and me walking up Yonge Street through the five o'clock rush, grabbing pizza slices to catch the early show at the Carlton. Eraserhead. Ran. Koyaanisqatsi. They looked happy and, I thought—just before I was crushed—that any moment can lead to anywhere.

This early morning, an hour before dawn, the house is dark, windows black, porch askew with strollers and jolly jumpers, car seat in the SUV. I want to leave petals, or oranges, something to tell them it's okay. Though I know it isn't okay. I want to leave ashes, warnings. My blue sweater. But even my thoughts are an intrusion, so I wander home, leaving them sleep, their pasts undisturbed.

Somewhere on the way home, from a different house, another baby cries and my belly aches to it, molecular memory, and I'll be falling, again, soon.

After I left, I didn't know who I was, what I was. Even supposing I could walk, could do the most basic things, I did not know what I was anymore. But I could not do the most basic things. Sleeping and eating were like dragging cats out of a pipe. They would not move and came only on their own time, with little mercy. Mrs. Thompson took care of my money, the landlord; she brought tea and milk and bread, and told me when the money was getting low. I didn't know who I was so I started where girls start when they drop out of school, where single mothers start when their kids start school, where old women start when their pensions cover the cost of food or rent, not both. This could be anywhere,

but for me it was the coffee shop, night shift on weekends, slipping into a full work week.

When I arrive home, Mrs. Thompson has left already,
leaving the porch light on. I click it off as I pass through
the hall and open the door to what I've become. Shaking
the bag of crunchies at the back door, I wait for Mr. Grey.
He can hear it from miles away, or, I think, he's followed
me all night, a few steps behind, and waits now, dragging
it out, making me wait, as cats do. He waddles up, barely
makes the rail and the balance to the sill. As he crunches
away I gently check out his belly, and realize he's not a
mister at all. The bag of crunchies has become, long ago,
a necessity, a promise, rather than a treat.

Mrs. Thompson's feet clunk down the stairs. My head turns just quick enough to see The Grey's tail disappear into the kitchen. She taps at the door, a light hesitant sound, repeating softly, so that it's near to a scratching.

"Do you have your cheque? I'm going now."

I scramble for pen and pad, peep around the near-closed door.

"I'm not decent," I try to smile, holding my arm stretched into the hall. She takes my cheque.

Something that happened there, that might be the worst moment, or just one in a series of bad, but something here that stands from the rest. He moved across the room, as he'd done, but his face was not his face.

I lurched for the door, my hands grabbing air to pull me forward, out. I saw the grow lights in the next room, the soft glow, flash of pink and red.

Then he jumped, coming up in front of me, a black wall breathing hard. Stopped. There was a stunned moment where we faced each other, just there.

Stopped. Slow.

Then movement, speed.

I dropped my body on the floor.

And the room disappeared.

He lunged. I scuttled down. He moved forward, groping, jabbing, trying to get whatever part of my body he could get hold of, and I moved backward, dragging my torso along by the heels of my hands. My arms wrenched backward, my legs trying to protect the points of contact.

The idea and concept of 'room' disappeared.

He shouted, repeated, "I'll kill you."

And I did believe him.

By the time I reached the other wall, I was attempting to reject the physical and conceptual world. Reason crumbled into sensation. I recognized my body on the floor, staring blankly ahead, flailing its hands in front of its face, babbling, unable to put two syllables together. I heard him in the distance. Saw his feet and legs peripherally. He told me to get up, but every part of me was intent on this rejection.

My body continued to flail and babble but in the end it was not successful because when he pulled his belt out—I saw the curve of his body, his heels lifting from the floor, the line of his legs arcing backward into his torso, the lift of his arms high over his head—and raised it to strike me, it flinched. My body responded, like an animal.

He laughed, hard and loud.

My first thought was a compound. *Danger crazy.*

I moved, crawled into the corner and huddled there.

He pointed his arm straight at me and the corner.

"Sit!" he shouted, and walked away. The door shut. Clank of the lock. The light gone out. Sit.

The room *disappeared*. The idea of room disappeared. Something in this moment.

I believe the psyche has a size, that there are widths and depths to it, dimensions; and that it is malleable, shrinks and grows according to what is placed there. Everything that had happened up to then had stretched me far but this moment told me something. Said something, more particular, more far, much bigger. But I don't know what.

I picture a disk floating in the mind, a glass disk of uneven thickness, awkward shape, that drifts in the mind, glinting, illuminating sense and memory; a disk that follows the focus of attention even in wandering daydream, nightdream; a disk that is the girl 'Magda' who sees the entire world but sees only through the aperture of this lens. Her eyes move and the lens moves. She thinks and the lens shapes her thoughts. She speaks and her words lift off from its smooth uneven surface. When she sleeps the disk drifts wide, sails currents, gathering mystery in darkness. In this particular moment—when the room disappears, and the idea of room disappears—the lens shifts just enough for me to catch it side-on rather than full; just enough for me to be looking at it rather than through it. Enough for me to see, there, that the lens exists and I am not the world, not the sun. There is the idea of room, the idea of Magda. Perception shifts from the disk to the substance within which the disk floats. Disjuncture.

It is an internal thing, an inner structure and event, which has as much to do with Mr. Kennedy as an accident has to do with the shape of a headlight.

It is July and it is hot. Around the back porch day lilies are blooming, sharp, alongside the late purple phlox, the burnt-out bergamot planted in too-bright sun. They bloom quickly and burn out in days.

At the bottom of my mind, when everything was broken and admitted, a back-load of endorphins kicked in. For an hour or two I was enraptured in the vibrant harmony of mystics. From the banks of the river, on the ground, by the water, willows swept the current as it passed, dragon-flies hummed their blue-stick way, fish glided in never-ending straights. I walked, my body deep with light, along the shore into the wood, the ravine. The wall of green became clear as I moved, separated into paths, serrated into leaf and branch, stem and blade. With an endorphin-rich clarity every blow, defense, and mistake fell into place within an active harmony which meaning could not be grasped, but was assured.

The squeaking under the back porch tells me The Grey has had her litter. I don't go near but listen as I kneel a few feet away, tearing blocks of sod in a semicircle from the fence, bringing sheep shit and compost and moss, turning the thing over until the clay-balanced dirt turns into rich black soil. Mrs. Thompson brings water with almond extract, a tall cold glass that looks milky but drinks clear and sweet.

"It's so good that you're doing this. Such a good yard, to go to waste all these years."

"Ah," she says as the soil turns black. "When the Russians took over the western countries, they took the topsoil from the Ukraine. Truckloads and truckloads off the land into their country. Black like velvet. Soft, you've never seen. Rich like butter."

In my hands lumps crumble into soft grain. The trowel cuts a small valley, a spiral out from centre. Seeds that might as well be invisible for their size, dropped and covered. Pumpkin. Radish. Lettuce. Peas along the fence. The seedlings come up in a speckled green spiral, tangle and overgrow the base. The Grey stretches out from under the bottom step, her floppy belly drags. The mewing gets louder, panicked, but she makes no mind moving up the path, leaves her back legs behind to stretch along the warm stone. Yawns, blinks, sleeps. I haven't been getting my regular complement of sparrows for awhile.

Inside my rooms I wash my black hands in the kitchen. The walls are grey with built-up dust, sticky with cobwebs. The stainless steel sink is not so stainless:

brown and yellow. I notice the corners, the ceilings, for the first time, brown, not with spills and stains but with the slow low sediment of living every day. Tiny amber cusps of water stains cover the ceilings and walls, layered from one steaming kettle after another. The dust that comes from this old house, like the respiration of age, joints settling, plaster weighing itself down, wood beams losing root-moisture, becoming brittle, becoming more dust. I think of myself on that balcony, a single rectangle of a room painted white on white, my skirts and blouses purchased crisp and new, unfolding scentless from the bag to cover a skin elastic, smooth, firm. I am beginning again, and who can tell what the body holds. I never did buy a broom or a mop, just used the one in the shed, worn down to a nub, and rags from a torn-up sheet. There is a scratching in the cupboard over the sink. Pushing aside five boxes of instant oatmeal, three boxes of Red Rose tea—jumbo size, 170 bags in each, on sale, then, for two-ninety-nine—I find mouse droppings and neatly emptied packets. I haven't been eating much. I notice my hunger, now, along with the walls, and vomit into the sink.

Wake Again

The evening will turn—it will turn—into midnight, and midnight will turn into morning, the women arriving for the next shift. I'll count the cash in the back room, at the small tin desk, between the racks of raw dough, shaped and waiting to be dunked into oil, bubbling up at their arrival; tipped onto their backs, scooped out into racks again, dripping, drying, spread with maple or chocolate, or glazed. The bills in my hands, counting five, ten, twenty; and twenty, forty, sixty. Tallying up between the register tape, and the float, cash and coins listed in their multiple values on deposit slips, cash receipts, tucked in, banded round, dropped into the slot in the safe where, if I've made a mistake—remember as I'm walking home or just falling into sleep, jerking awake, saying Damn! to the air—it will be kept, held, uncorrectable, sitting in the dark in the safe, a rectangle of grey light steady in the steel dark, casting light on these bundles, and mine, the one with the mistake, waiting to be found out when the boss's wife comes on Thursdays with her twirl of correct numbers, her heavy keys, the one that fits before the combination, the one that fits after. She puts the canvas banking bag open on the floor in front of the door, reaching in a whole arm, scooping twenty-one bundles—one for every shift every day, the thickness or thinness telling exactly the shift, night, day, afternoon—they fall into the mouth of the bag and the door swings wider, her head goes in, out, in, hand reaching for strays, then a key, the click and whirl, and another key. The rope that weaves in and out of the steel loops, the mouth pulled tight, squished into folds, wrinkles; and the metal clasp that pulls down the rope, tight to the folds, that locks again, so that the bag, if grabbed, lost, stolen, will be a bugger to open, not impenetrable, but the canvas, the lock, will put up resistance, the prize won't be easy, there'll be time to track it down.

She stops to place the canvas bag into a plastic shopping bag, doubled up, a trick she learned as a child, then hangs it off her wrist, walks around the donut kitchen, behind the counter, not saying a word, making the women nervous, looking over their shoulders, watching them count payments and change, count donuts into bags and boxes. Don't give them napkins unless they ask, she says. Don't hand out the fresh ones until the day-olds are done. Don't bake the double-chocolate anymore—they're not selling. Okay. Okay, Miss. Yes. But Margie will make a small batch, a smaller batch, for the lady who comes in every morning at quarter past nine, who asks for a large tea, double-milk, teabag in, and a double-chocolate donut, the only ones sold; who doesn't have to ask anymore because it's been years and years of the same routine, the same tea, the same donut, the same smile between them now, which is warm as old friends, as bright, as warm, as if they had grown up together on the same street, played in the same park, met before school to walk, after school to talk, read the same books, struggled through the same lessons, crushed on the same boys as their bodies developed into the curves they would become, have to live with forever, it seemed, until the hormones shifted again, and the curves would droop, expand outward, downward, becoming something else again. They smiled like that, every morning, but had never talked, did not know names or lives or worries, careers or entertainments; the heartbreak that can set you back decades, the intimacies that can open the universe into stardust and travel, the horizon pushed back, opened up, so you can see that all your dreams are possible, and that dreams breed dreams, exponential expansion, and these new dreams are possible too, heart-children, that push back horizons, of joy and sorrow, pleasure and pain, opens up the mind, the soul, the heart beating wild, and confident, so confident within this intimacy, as long as you don't look back, look down, look too casually at his eyes, her eyes, to see, to see: we're ordinary. Our pasts have shaped us into our lives, our bodies have drawn limits around our vision, our possibility. When I wanted only work, only school, I was aiming too low. I should have wanted CEO, professorship, world renowned expert. I should have wanted love. Where did it go now? I looked too close. I looked too deep. I did not look far enough. And the lady smiles at Margie, pays the correct change, drops a quarter in the tip box, and the next person steps up as she steps away, turns from the counter, almost bumps the boss's wife who is ready to go now, after collecting the cash, asserting her presence; she steps back behind the counter, through the kitchen, past the safe so silent now, empty, dark inside where the grey rectangle of light illuminates only softly the perfect planes of a perfect impenetrable cube, the thin rectangle of light, sharp at the centre, brings a secondary light, shadows in the darkness.

Is it foolish, at my age, to ask, where are my dreams, what has happened to my dreams?

A steady rain pours from the sky, muted streets slick with shine. The movement of seeds dropping, gathering at puddles to gutter from pipe to stream to lake. My feet slap through the downpour, soaking through, skin. The hard callouses that form at the edge of the heel, the tip of the long toe, the inner ball of the foot, soften into white, become so tender there is a grittiness in every step, chafing against sock, rubbing layers raw. It is falling and I am falling with it. The run-off from the streets, ankle high, flows south along the shape of the earth, to the parks along the flood plain. Water flows over the saturated grass, creating streams above ground, parks become riverbeds and rivers overflow, the surface level nudging up, flooding the burrows of small creatures, carrying them away. Birds cling to high branches until the river tips the trees away, then they head inland, away from their nests, into high buildings and roofs where they'll wait it out while their feather-less peers float down in the rush, marooned on a log, carried off to meet new streams on the grasslands which have become shallow rivers. The main river, indistinguishable from the run-off, churns brown, thick, roiling at narrow passages where rock and shale climb steep, narrow, shaping the water deep and wild, pulling trees whole from the ground. It reaches up to ground level, climbs to touch the steel girders of the overpass, the sky. Concrete pillars bearing the weight, now, not only of freight trains and cross-country tours but also the push and rush of tons of water—only water—coming down too much, too fast. Taking a beating from the side, from the north, where memory lives, stays put if it can, or breaks out, pushing against the architecture. The white-wash paint is sanded down, chipped at. Grains of sand loosen from the cement mix; bits of gravel chip off, become debris for the next bridge or tree, carried to the mouth of the river. Then the imperceptible; a slight irrelevant incongruity in the make that would have held strong for decades becomes a fault, a crack, a loosening. Everything above and below holds steady in the predicted uniform strength, but this lisp, this sag, this jag of near-weakness becomes weakness, fault.

It shifts.

The overpass pulls over from straight, the top part moving downriver, the down part holding true. The river rushes at the embedded steel cables, they twist, and the rails bend. And bend, into the touch, and sink under the touch—a coolness there, a warmth, a pull alien to its hard life, its suspension in air, this wetness, movement, which is of cold and heat, but textured, too, touch, a caress, an embrace, a submergence. Collapse. This entity that has lain below, a brown ribbon sparkling in sun, freezing into grey, drifting into white landscape while the rail hung, black and black and black against the sky; shining sometimes in the glaze of rain; covered sometimes, also, a white grid laid against the sky, bends now, met by something equal and different, converged. This hard journey from ore shafts, mazed deep and low in the earth, rock crated in networks of carts that fill and roll in the light of helmet-lamps (hands—were there hands? Human hands? Warmth, grip, articulation. Will.) through shafts and levels, steep inclines to the surface pit gouged into the earth; trucked across highways to the forge melting rock into liquid, shapeless (ah, it remembers: to be liquid, shapeless, red), then mixed and poured into shape, frozen thin, stretched into beams, bolted straight onto the ground. (Oh, to remember the ground, the earth, the deep, snug, silent, dark. Black, safe, gathered, clustered into time, settled in, settled together, settled. Home.) Bending as the pillars break, dipping, equal at last to the pull.

I was trying so hard to behave, believing that, if I did behave, if I reached back, he would see past himself, past what he was doing; believing that he would see me, Magda; a girl, I believed, he had loved. I would act, argue, respond, argue, comply, protest, all in the hope, the faith, that he would see—that he could—and let me go.

Some of these mornings, the feel of the balcony years, the first adult-me standing in a bare room above the city. Classical on CJRT, though I didn't know what it meant at all; eight o'clock news from the BBC, getting dressed in those skirts and blouses, tea of course; the balcony, the sun, the city. The light. And—I didn't know—it was ordinary. And quite fine. I could feel myself there, my existence, real existence, in the ordinary morning; feel the mask, I thought, of my clothes, my job. And the realness of the sun rising on the city, and of my life rising too. Like television, I was real.

Not in the long empty nights, but in the mornings, with work clothes, my tea, my bare apartment, the city very beautiful from the eighth floor. The trees of Allan Gardens, the lower buildings outside the city core, and the core city, office towers huddled in the southwest in jagged height, light blanching their eastern walls, brilliant, black on the west side. Music playing that I didn't understand or appreciate, wordless. No television then. The music in the room, flowing through, unrecognized, like rain, in the background.

I'm standing at the window, watching the rain soak the ground. At the subway on mornings, the ticket-taker rarely looked up. His grey hair bowed to the counter as we went by, turnstile clicking, tickets dropping. He was counting tickets, counting change, making piles for the usual requests for five or ten or twenty, for convenience, when someone asked in the morning rush. But he was not looking up. If I stopped and asked for tickets, I had to repeat, lean close and repeat, because he was in his glass cubicle, busy making everything ready for passengers who do ask. Two small television monitors, black and white, with a view of each platform, eastbound, westbound, unwatched for morning rush hour because the crowds are there, on the platform, and it is safe in a crowd, we are all safe; coming from our windows, our homes, stepping into the morning route, walking down our small streets, past houses so familiar but new, each morning, as the slant of the sun shifts, from the tight little white sphere in the northeast at winter to the blazing red of an August sun, the earth tilting away from the sun just when the orbit comes closest. And the light on the street—eight thirteen a.m. straight through the year, every morning the same, so the light touches the street, the houses, the trees, a few minutes different every day; shifting in the increment of moments, from brilliant to shade to brilliant. Just when you most need a shaded morning walk, when the night has dripped itself out of your skin with heat, cool baths every half-hour, powdered sheets to absorb the damp, waking as groggy as you slept, then sunlight making its way up the shaded step, touches your foot, your knee, your lap with pure yellow heat. Solstice. Equinox. Moments that passed me by, went unnoticed until now, when, for nine years, the street is the same street, the houses the same houses, the routine the same. In the house down the street, blocks over, as I prepare now for sleep, Louis will be waking fully, up and bright first thing, no need for coffee or cigarettes or stimulants. His engagement with the world is assertive, aggressive. He knows that sleep is a waste of time, a waste of mind. It's consciousness, awareness, awakeness that's real, that's true. He'll unhook a white shirt from a row of white shirts, drape the white cotton over the ironing

board, and press out every rift of material creating an
unplanned, unwilled, ragged crease of shadow in the
sharply tailored design. Collar stiff, smooth, button too
close to the neck, because he's gained a little weight, just
a little; lifting his arms into the swoop of material, the
blaze of white arcing down, around, up and over his back,
an office matador to the blur of shadows in the room.
Grey-black-blue pants, carefully folded to crease, all the
white cotton scrunched and tucked, smoothed over his
hips, zipped, buttoned down—this line, clear line, pant-
line from ankle to hip to waist, that shows no body, then
the bloom of white cotton, hiding the contours of his
chest, draped from the slope of shoulders, wrapped tight
around the neck. He'll stand now, the full length mirror
wide, picking a ribbon of silk from a hundred ties—this
thin stripe of expression against the uniform, light blue,
dark blue, medium blue, maroon, yellow, all dotted or
striped or sprinkled with tiny insignia, a fingernail boat
or cap or bug, diamonds, squares, spheres transversed
by arcs—pulled round his shoulders, his neck, tucked
under and knotted: at the throat this trim perfect knot
lying at the base of suit and skin.

He is there, over there, dressing his dressings as he
did, year after year, when I was there; when, on Thursday mornings, I could forego the skirts, the blouses,
watch him dress from our bed, because I'd be pulling on
a pair of jeans, a sweatshirt, a stack of books, catching
the subway north, opposite the morning rush into town;
catching the bus at Wilson Station, wending through
wide residential streets to the campus where I'd step off
the bus into a wasteland of green fields and parking lots.
Step down off the curb, onto the path, the bus emptying
with me, stop by stop as it looped around the campus

from social science, to physical science, business studies, to fine arts. Buildings corralled in the centre, grey
monolithic things that would have passed unnoticed at
the centre of the city, stand out here, wall flowers at the
dance, plunked down, connected up haphazard, no plan,
it seems, the ugliest building beside the most beautiful,
dark hallways a turn from bright courtyards, a grand central foyer flanked by rows of windowless cell-like rooms.
I believed, in this setting of chaos attempting to be order that I had arrived at the centre of things. Sitting in
plastic chairs lined around cement walls, blackboards
layered with the ghosts of lessons, explications, explanations, presentations of bits of knowledge scrawled in
sentence or formula one row to the next; my notebooks
filling with script, line after line, page after page, textbook
after textbook with the centre of things, the map, the
place from which every human thing could be planned
and followed. Taking the elevators up floor after floor
of books, the library was its own building, packed tight
with paper, shelf after shelf on floor after floor, computers throwing up name after name if you typed anything
in—say, fork, or frog, or god—the titles would ream off,
line by line, screen by screen, and I'd be printing down
rows of numbers on scraps of paper, numbers cryptic
to any sane mind, but here they were definite, specific,
particular, a code as clear as tulips and the varieties of
red. Sitting cross-legged at the foot of a shelf—at the
RC701s for example, or the LX103s—the titles played
off each other, each leading to the one beside but slanting, slightly, as they went, so that, by the end of the rack,
they would have moved from Colonialism to colony,
Bach to Beethoven, Kafka to Kant if you went along far
enough, all in the smallest, often most unlikely, possible

steps. This is how the world is mapped—experience, ideas, emotion, actions—all mapped in these rooms and floors, so I could believe that everything was possible. There would be no need now for death wishes, boredom, despair. No need for questions, for getting lost, for being trapped anywhere, because the map was here, duplicated and extended in libraries across the globe, the answer must be here. It could only be looking, looking hard enough, looking well enough. My fingers skipped through the pages of the anthropology texts, lifting pages, my eyes skipped through sentences, lifting words, details, ideas; feeling, finally, that the whole world had been given to me, and there would be no need of falling.

He'd be tucking his billowing white shirt into his blue pants, a blue so dark it presented as black, discernable as blue only in full direct daylight.

I'd haul books home, scoop up words, paragraphs words as I sat at the kitchen counter, not knowing, not comprehending, not making the leap, the connection, that behind each book—each one—there is a life, a woman, a man, the universe of sensation inside, the subtleties of experience, teeth-brushing, love making, doubt.

I did not realize that the map, though large, book by book, is inadequate to pain. That, maybe, the reason for the largeness is pain.

He'd be tucking in his white shirt, and I'd be watching from the bed, with an absolute belief in the totality of what we were, of what I'd become. And, on the way to work or school, at the subway, I'd ask for ten adult tickets, and have to repeat the request each time, because the ticket-taker was engaged, absorbed, in preparing for the request, his grey head bowed to the counter, the tickets torn into cards of two by five, the last pair bent to fold along the perforation so that it would tear off easily in the morning rush.

That was ordinary, and extraordinary, to me.

At any given office, on any given day, the women are gathered round their desks, waiting for love. I gathered with them there, believing I was different, that I would make my own life, be my own person, attend university, get promoted into wealth, safety, security, without the need of marriage. But this was not true. My heart, buried deep, chained silent behind the deepest door, wanted only love. The rest was bunk, foolish, external things; attractive to a possible mate but having within themselves no sense, no necessity, no substance. No ground. No anchor in the body of life. Love, intimacy, touch. I put on my skirts and blouses, wore pantyhose through the sweltering summer, high heels in the ice and snow, pinned my hair up from my face where the curve of my jaw arced softly to my cheek, my mouth, my hazel eyes that could be mistaken for green if he wanted, or not. When I was promoted to file clerk I learned my first lesson in the indexing of details. The filing system, a relic from the eighteenth century, thirteenth century, where every memo would be classified to any subject to which it might pertain—the skill of guess work, the subtleties of knowing who might be looking for what in any particular future—the main location chosen, and index cards of five or six or ten, typed up and kept in an alphabetical file box that stood at the front of the shelves, in a primary spot, directly under the white fluorescent, in tin slats that pulled out flat and long, cards feathered down, flipping up to read, then flipped down, tucked neat, disappearing in the bulk of the steel cabinet. Coming from chaos, I was delighted, soothed, calmed, going through

my stacks of memos, letters, magazines, finding a place
for each, leaving notes wherever I thought people might
look. Notes to say: It's here, over here, a few rows left of
what you thought, a few shelves down from what you believed, a few files higher then what you planned.

I'm standing this morning at the front window, dressed
in my favourite black wool pants, my square-toed shoes,
black tight turtleneck; watching the rain, the puddles on
the street, hearing it under the Beethoven sonatas, smoking cigarettes still despite health warnings and public
contempt; standing at the window. And I am ordinary.
It is ordinary. Inside the beat of life. (Seeds, here, pulled
down by the rain, off branches. Damping, swelling,
dropping into puddles and gutters, flowing, transported,
spread to far places. The shore, lake, shore. The seeds
of this maple growing in Niagara, Buffalo, Kingston.)
The moment of breakfast, between sleep and the world,
when we're held cupped in our homes. Rested, fed, sheltered, about to leave, go into the streets, the buildings,
hallways, rooms, extra-necessary tasks; wearing the right
thing. The right pants, the right coat, the right umbrella.
The right change for the bus, subway, streetcar. The right
silence, in this moment, suspended between sleep and
the world, night dreams and day plans, suspended. A
moment's respite here. A moment's pause.

How ordinary and wonderful it was for me to be
there, beginning my own life—the harshness, I know,
the hyper-focus, the coldness. But. Okay—beginning
my life after the wreck. It's where the ordinary becomes
wonderful. The routine of it, the rhythm of it, finally begins to click back in. Disaster cleared out of my heart so
I can hear this again, feel it, like the rain in constant wet,

the way it's under everything, comforting, beautiful, wet.
Glowing. Moving.

The children trail off to school, streets filling with odd pairs, triplets, quints; pink and orange packs hanging from their shoulders, small umbrellas with snouts and ears, their runners splashing the rain, stepping over fat flood-ousted worms, assuming the ground. The street empties and the last child leaves her house, hair tousled, clothes unkempt, tugging the straps of her pack over her shoulders as she half-runs, but doesn't run because, really, she is still asleep, though her eyes are open, though her body is moving, tugging on the pack, though she is rushing for the yard, the bell she'll be late for, she is asleep and won't wake until mid-afternoon, after lunch, and television, and walking slowly back to school, singing softly the theme from her favourite show, trailing her fingers along the fences—wire, iron, wood—and hedges—cedar, hemlock, boxwood—as she meanders back to the schoolyard, the bell, her seat. I turn away from the window, pull the zipper at my throat down the front of my uniform, a woven plastic material that resists liquid, spills spill off and run down in rivulets to the floor. The uniform opens down, zipper unclipped at the bottom. I shrug it off, hang it beside the other one, on a hanger, so it won't wrinkle. The mattress on the floor begs me to sleep, and I lay, listening to the rain.

Mrs. Thompson clunks down the steps, out the door, and I fade, nod, fade, the steady drop of rain shaped by the push of wind, a pattering against leaves, glass, tin that comes in, fades out, comes in.

I wish I had an heroic deed or a baby, but what I have are three near-blind kittens groping under the stairs; one then another then the next, finding the path out, blinking in the first scent of sky and grass before loping over to harass The Grey. I've pretty much fire-bombed my rooms, chemically speaking, with bleach and ammonia and Comet, painted every inch in yellow and green; so much so that the poor cat won't come in, not even to the window sill, but sits on the railing by the door waiting for her dishes of food, the kittens below pouncing at the bend of every blade of grass. I've started eating again   oh potatoes, eggs, carrots—and discovered that you can't actually live on the wages of a coffee shop clerk. Rent, soap, a bag of cat food and that's about it. Margie laughs when I say it, Welcome to the real world, girl. And gives me one of the day-olds. But how does she do it? Seven shifts a week, spare bucks from her parents, basement apartments and food banks. There's a difference between humility and humiliation, arrogance and pride, and the need of food is at the border there. I take on two double shifts, meet the daytime crowd, the soup and sandwich people, milk and juice, for lunch and dinner. The after-school kids with their two-hour cokes. On some days, as they come in, the kids and clerks, cops and road workers, women and men, I find that I am no longer afraid of or for them. I find myself chatting, laughing, knowing their preferences by their faces, knowing that little piece of routine from their days, little by little realizing that I have become myself again.

The morning after I used the roach chalk, as I went, in shadow, from bed to bathroom, the floor crackled under my bare feet, stiff bodied shells inanimate. One day I read a paper and I do not cry. I try it again a week later and I'm fine. A few months later it's a regular routine and I try a book. Cognitive functioning. I am able to think again.

Solitude

I'm not sure I believe in capitalists but they do believe in themselves, which is how we make the world. Any grain of doubt is a killer. I've walked over to Dufferin from Bathurst because the Dufferin bus goes all the way south, only dropping in at the subway rather than stopping to empty itself of passengers and loop back up. The subway is faster but, having worked nights for seven years, I enjoy the daylight along the way. My body is starved for it, so I take the Dufferin bus, transfer at Queen to the Long Branch car, rumble and slide through daylight all the way, sun creeping up at the lake, light reaching slant across the passengers' backs, travelling counter to the downtown crowds. I'm working two jobs for awhile, nervous about letting go of one before the other is secure, making a little extra money for awhile but I'll have to give it up soon. Don't have the energy I once did. Money has become important suddenly, as I've gotten older. Love, peace, and justice don't get you very far when your body breaks down. I have more sympathy for greed.

The buses arrive in packs of three or four, all clumped together from the daily jam of morning traffic. The first two sail past without stopping and there's always one or two people on the sidewalk scrambling and angry, though we know there's another one or two just out of sight at the dip of the overpass, or the top of the hill. Cold morning to wait long standing, the April chill still in the morning even after a warm week. We still have a few blizzards before spring, though we forget it every year, how long the winter lingers.

I let the third bus take most of the passengers, let it sail off. The fourth and fifth come butt to face like two cars on a train, each of them full enough but more empty than the others. I sit in my favourite seat, the last double before the rear doors, by the window, facing away from the too-bright sun, lightly hypnotized by the passing flow of sidewalk and curb.

My new job is with a new company, seven people working in a small room, flushing into success with an internet service that's going great guns. We're tucked into a storefront at Lakeshore and Twelfth Street. This is my family neighbourhood, though I haven't been back for twenty years or so. The streetcar screeches in and out of the Humber loop, a throw-back of a way station, sunk into the bowl of three overpasses, with a tiny brick station house encircled by streetcar rails. This had been as far as we could go as kids, before looping back into the home territory of our little piece of the city. The car screeches into and out of the tunnel, the overpass for the expressway, then we're riding the last straight arm of rail, a lost bit of branch, into what was once cottage country to a horse-drawn town.

It's strange for me to think that it existed before I did, has its own history; that my family was not the first family to live here with the rest of the people brought in to fulfill the necessities of neighbourhood. Stretching three miles—about five kilometres now—along the lake front, moving from house to park, store to lake, it seemed like the whole world and more. There could be no good reason to leave, no good reason to live anywhere else. From here it looks charming, run down, not a Starbucks in sight—so blessed that way. I get off at the Twelfth Street stop, in front of where the old Goodyear Rubber and Tire Factory used to be, United Rubber Workers Local 677. It's a co-op development now, all the rubber dust and machines plowed under and hauled away. As I step off the streetcar, the sky opens up. I can smell the lake. Nostalgia is embedded in the air here, sunk into the pavement along with the spills from old ice creams and pop cans.

I wanted this job because this is where I started and, through a breaking of the mind, I have to start again. I thought if I came to this place, lived in this place, I might be able to put the pieces together, make a story of it, something that flows in a direct line across a landscape rather than the disembodied fragments I'm used to.

I'm the only clerk in a gaggle of techies. No one is in yet so I stand at the edge of the piles of papers they've accumulated since they started the business. I'm sure they used a dump truck to haul these papers over here; and the same truck to tip them through the front door. There are a few piles in the rubble but mostly it is separate leaves of paper scattered as sure as autumn, and tipped across tables and floors. I ordered two good-sized filing cabinets. They're sure to arrive any day now. I wade through the mess, plant myself in a corner and start sorting, piling, sorting, getting into a rhythm of hand and eye that is hypnotic, calming in the way that shelling peas or shucking corn is calming.

I never left the basement. The light and dirt piled into me, forming a moat around my inner heart, sheltering my outer mind from memory. I lived as two complex halves and might have been able to create, from the outer half, a life almost complete in its humanness. But the inner half was wanting; aching, following the moves of my life with anguish while I glided surface deep; responding, unknown to me, to every love and heartbreak, taking it in without expression, filling up, pushing against the dirt and light until a fissure formed, seeping half into half, the two lives and times, meeting each other, memory to memory. Time folded in on itself so both occurred at once in the same body. Body struggling against mind: sense against experience, present against past.

Two months ago when I was shoveling the front walk, Mrs. Thompson collapsed in my arms, her grocery oranges rolling down the front path stopping solid in the new snow on the sidewalk. In the hospital, her trolley tucked into a corridor, she confesses. I was there, she says. I was in the camps. My hands wrapped around the claw of her grasp. Her eyes blue with terror. I took the soil. The nurses and doctors squeeze by with charts and wheelchairs and gurneys. Her eyes tilt up, lids closing into coma. Later, when she woke, her son took her to live with his family in Brampton. I wonder if her confession saved her life or caused her paralysis, or if it did nothing at all.

Morning, early morning now, I take a coffee and the bus down to the lake a few minutes before dawn. Going against the first straggle of rush hour traffic, heading outward while everyone else makes their way inward, to the centre of town, the buildings there, the activity; commerce and art tucked into a small square of land, the collection of bodies, people, creating their own gravity by the multiplicity of their presence. Everyone goes there. Everyone. And so: everyone goes. Then buses are needed, another streetcar line, a new subway looping up and down and up. I ride along Dupont until it splits, take the subway to High Park, through the hills and trees, around the big pond, follow Lakeshore to Park Lawn, Mimico, Long Branch. My heart is still not with me, so when the streets become familiar, when we cross the overpass and I get off the streetcar, walk the turn into the long curve of asphalt to the parking lot at the tip of the lake, I'm filled with a familiarity that feels foreign, so long gone. Before the storm, there were streets here, small houses, cottages, but the land here is part of the floodplain and got wiped out. The city bought it up, made it a public park. I sit facing the lake, body open to the cool night air. In the grey light, the earth turns toward the sun, light catches the bellies of gulls, a terrific white defined against their shadowed backs. I wander to a nook and fall asleep to this sound, a cry for food, for scraps, whatever will keep them alive, turning.

Then I go home. Find myself on the bus again, or at the coffee shop, or at the office; sitting lulled, unpacking boxes

of cups, discussing software with the girls. In these interactions, small connections, the daily routines of almost-
touch between strangers who become familiar, become
human to me now, fragile not threat, what I am begins
to become—faintly, faintly—more than one man slam-
ming one door shut.

We sit around the table in the back room, Roger, standing at the front, articulates the vision, the plan for the future of the company. The red dry-erase marker squeaks
across the white surface, a tin cylinder of liquid pressing out with the pressure of his hand, trail of liquid that
turns to dust almost immediately on leaving the felt tip.
He stands easily in front of the staff, wearing jeans today
because it is vision day, planning day. Mounds of donuts
have been picked up, laid out; coffee perked and poured
into the large thermos. There will be lunch later, a tray
each of sandwiches, vegetables, desserts delivered from
around the corner, paid for by the company; a perk, it
seems, for staff, that indicates generosity and, also, that
we are trapped here for the day, not allowed to leave, not
to break into our own time this whole day, not to take
a walk at lunch down these residential streets, houses
mostly empty because everyone's at work, away; walk
down to the bottom of the street where the asphalt
meets grass, a small park at the lake; three pipes planted
in the ground between curb and green, to step around,
heels pressing holes into the ground, sit primly on an
envelope to protect my work clothes, on a rock by the
waves.

Roger outlines the process for the day in erasable
script, a process he took from his own seminar, week-
long retreat, leadership training at the Banff Centre for
Management Arts, where he sat at the tables, watching
the team of consultants play off each other like water—
Mike and Jim from Montana; four-inch binders distributed around the room contain everything that will be

said this week; reproduce every slide, every white board, every flip chart, precisely, exactly, because this is not science, not complex, it is management, leadership, how to rouse employees to enthusiasm, bonding devotion to the goals of the company because the goals of the company are the goals of the person; we all want to contribute to the good of the world by being the best we can be, don't we? Take care of our homes, our families, buy that hot sports car along the way. We are on the same road here, going in the same direction, on the same team. Roger loves the application of theory, knowledge, to everyday life: this is where all the talk becomes real. Small deep thrill when he takes something he's learned and places it into action, delighted every time it works, back to the books if it doesn't. Knowledge is not abstract to him, not some lah-de-dah, hoity thing to be kept in libraries and colleges, but the meaningful application of thought to life to thought. Astonishment every time.

In the Banff session room, listening, listening, mountains hanging in the background out the window, a shadow of rock lurking against the sky, which he found, in the end, frightening. He didn't like going outside there, walking the tilting paths from bedroom to dining room to bar. His shoulders scrunched up, he hunched over, protecting his belly from the weight of the mountains, the constant reprimand of his smallness, the campus buildings becoming fragile, perched on a small piece of the slope of this mass. He did more than well at the exercises, concentrating exquisitely on the task at hand so that he wouldn't have to look up, see the giants smirking around, crowding in, delaying the sun by hours, taking it away too soon, with their bulk and peaks. He presents it here with an ease and security that speaks as much to his relief at not being in the mountains as it does to his mastery of the material. He loosens up the staff by a free-fall brainstorm on good communication, notices that Jasmine is drifting away, not participating, doodling on her note pad, and asks her to please come up and list key values on the flipchart paper.

Jasmine smiles, saunters to the easel, picks up a fat blue marker, immediately feeling like eye-candy for a game show, something she always wanted to be, the smooth-water flow-line of an evening gown mid-morning, big smile, the gesture of knee and hip and arms arcing wide, weightless from the shoulder, as if the real prize was not the new washer-dryer, not the ten thousand dollars, but her, the vitality she always felt inside, simmering, bubbling, ready to explode, flow, into the classroom, the streets; her father's lap where she sat sheltered every evening watching television skip from scene to scene, show to show, his hand warm on her knee, his chest holding her whole body, their mutual warmth creating an egg around them, like pregnancy. She watched as he fell to sleep, the *hunck-hunck-hunck* of his snores, until he woke, jerking, stretching into an arc, forgetting she was there, tipping her up and off to the side like a pony ride. She rolled with the tip, said *Dah-ddeeee*, and he'd pull her up, scratch his beard against her face and let her go with a tap on the butt. Bouncing down the hallway, into her bedroom, pulling her dolls, then her comic books, then her make-up from the top of her dresser, certain that, when she reached high-school, eighteen, twenty-one, she'd be the star, the angel, the girl she knew herself to be.

Roger says, "You can write that down."

We all sit straight-backed, trying to look alert, shifting our commuter-minds from our usual start-work-routine to Roger, his voice, his reasons. Everyone is a little dazed, hesitant to lift a cup or donut, in case caught out, but needing the caffeine, the sugar. For me it's a scene from a different life, except that I am not a primary person here, so I'm not jumpy. My concerns are elsewhere.

Day by day, month by month, I have begun to find my place in the world again. I watch, listen, try to re-learn the correct behaviours, interactions, wants, of normal people. Gesture, tone, mannerism. I pick up bits and pieces of their ways, trying to mimic—to shrug, giggle, roll my eyes, as people do—fit this together to a coherence. Hints, signs, pathways back to the ordinary.

People come to me. Maybe because I am watching, maybe because I don't speak much—what can I say?—maybe because I am empty and need to learn. People come. Roger on Mondays after lunch, Renada on Wednesday morning when everyone else is out, Omar on Wednesday afternoon just before closing, Jasmine regularly but unpredictably. I am sitting at my desk, quiet, my body bent over the stacks of envelopes or papers or bills, blue-stamping dates and times, hands shuffling whispers in the quiet lobby. They'll wander over. Maybe they pick up the stacks and start sorting to postal code, or replenish the second stapler, or just lean their body against the counter, half-slumped, and talk, friendly, easy, open. Through scraps of details building up over months, they tell me their lives, forming maps and shapes, depths that echo in their smallest gestures and mannerisms, the way they pronounce a vowel. A new layer of perception for me; I can see—in the way they speak, in the incoherence of the telling, from my own unknowing and knowing and unknowing again—that they are not aware of their own shape, the rivers that make their lives, bend it to and away from places they may never know the roots of. Forced to learn a shape I did not chose to know, I infer a scope in other peoples' lives; and, in doing so, become exiled from this sweet unknowing.

I do not know if I can fit again. Do not know if integration is possible, or if I will always slip between the interactions of people, acutely aware, always, that my nod and smile and *hiya*, however sincere, is not genuine but a ritual too heavily rehearsed, that I've learned and lost and re-learned. Acutely aware, always, that I am not mended, that I ever needed mending.

Roger says, "You can write that down. "

Jasmine uncaps the marker, sharp illicit scent, turns part-way to the paper and writes: *efficiency*, in small print letters across the paper. Miscalculating space, distance, length, the word starts full, spacious, then scrunches, veers off, slopes down as she sees she is approaching the end of the page and will not have enough room. She does better with: *professionalism, organization, courtesy*, but the first word sits there, dark blue on buff, a visual contradiction to its own meaning, most in-efficient, squished into a space which, she thinks, is just not big enough. She should have had more space. It does not have to be this shape, starting so well, then squeezing into this barely legible line. She should have given herself more space, instead of chasing after the captain of the football team. Oh, but he was so cute, so damn good-looking. And the way he looked at her, meeting her at the door of every class, taking her books from her arms—never mind that he was skipping his own education, a month away from

failing out. He was there, at the end of each class, waiting for her, nearly speechless with his want of her. This is
what she followed. And it's not bad. Not a bad life. Four
kids bam-bam-bam and they both have decent jobs and
here, here at work, at her job, she finds she can be the
game show hostess, can learn, as she's learning now, the
elements of business communication, the strength of
team work, the value of responsibility. And night-time,
his body. Warm, always warm. Deeper, so much more
surprisingly deeper, than any childhood dream.

The sandwiches come just as Roger is making a point
about the connection between all people. Over-step-
ping, he hauls the delivery man away from his delivery,
asks his name, puts an arm around his shoulders, and
says, "We're all in this together—isn't that true, Bill?"
Renada cringes, thinks, Jesus Christ, Roger, give it a
break. But says nothing. She wonders again about her
taste in lovers, and shrugs, again. She knows she needs
men she can control, men already committed to other
relationships, safe men. Devoted, dreamy-eyed hearts
so intent on making the world around them simple, at-
tainable, that they don't see their own lives. She wonders, again, if she should start therapy again, but, Jesus,
the pain. It was too much. On the brink of suicide for
two years and all he'd do is nod with sympathy and say,
It's part of the process, part of the healing. She thought,
fuck healing, then, and only started feeling better, sane,
after she stopped. True, she still couldn't sleep, often
spent weekends curled up on the floor beside her bed,
but that's what Roger was for. Roger and his kind, his
predecessors, her history, the history of her skin. It was
not sophisticated, her mind, her defenses; it was rudi-
mentary, a crude place of yes and no, me or you, kill

or die. She'd gotten that far at least, having some sense now for why she was always breaking up relationships, then leaving, losing interest, as soon as he choose her. Too bad. She felt no feelings, no sympathy, no remorse. That's the way the game is, boy. That's the game. She knows now that *it* isn't the way the game is. She knows that it's her, just her game, the way her game goes. So she doesn't press Roger, doesn't try to break up his marriage, gives just enough flack to keep the tension peaked, keep him in. She picks a plate from the stack, chooses tuna salad on dark rye, slices of sweet red pepper, and realizes, as he smiles at her, but doesn't look at her, from across the room, she realizes: He's got his game too.

They come. They speak. Maybe because I am quiet, maybe because I am empty, maybe because invisibility has become an essential skill and it is easy, so easy, to disappear under their lives. To become the woman in the lobby who nods and smiles and thanks you for your help. Disappearing under voices, disappearing under the work day. Disappearing under a culture that is, or presumes that everyone is, entirely safe.

I listen, grateful for the practice.

Renada realizes: He's got his game too.

And she stops, held still, holding a cup balanced on the edge of a plate of food, frozen there, on the edge of the widening of perception, the cliff of recognizing another person's life, another person's will. In a flash she remembers why she sleeps on the floor beside the bed when her mind dissipates into blackness and she is locked in the pain/ no-pain of feeling nothing. Each night her mother pulling her, the child Renada, down beside the bed onto the soft rag rug, rocking her in the cup of her crossed legs, whispering songs and stories, like prayers, twirling her hair into loose knots, untwirling, until Renada, her breath heavy with warmth, became her mother, and herself, the two of them a single name, connecting back centuries as the single action of embrace.

That was peace, love. She wonders if she was right to major in software programming, if she hadn't, after all, been seducing another kind of betrayal, one more personal, trapped by the power there, the illusion of power; trying, in the end, to track down her own power by participating in her own annihilation? This veering away from humanities into maths not because she loved math so much but because she knew it had oomph, status, a certain obscurity of agility that created a mysticism around it—all those numbers lined up across the board, layered symbols pulled in from ancient cultures, formulas layered by transverse lines, joined by a simple equal sign, two boards of blackboard, five pages of formula, balanced by two dashes, one atop the other, the small space in between, the huge space above and below. She had enjoyed it, genuinely so, but it wasn't love. She wonders if her direction had more to do with the surprise, slight awe, with which her teachers, the other students, held her when she wandered up to the board, whipped off the proof, the answer. Did direction have more to do with the response of strangers, more to do with the appearance of strength than with strength itself. Integrity. Finishing off her lunch, pushing the plate away, she becomes tired, wishing, with great sadness, that Roger had stayed true to his wife.

I listen, grateful for the practice. These shapes tumble in, too deep, too pressing, with too much meaning for a woman removed. I try to fit my shape beside theirs, a puzzle of gaps and spaces, ill-fit pieces touching at the odd tip of edges matched to colour but nothing else.

Are we all, then, feral kaleidoscopes, spinning wild webs that go anywhere, fit nowhere?

The meeting pushes on into late afternoon. Roger tapping away at the pages of his binder, careful not to miss the main points, developing the general guidelines into the specifics of a company plan, so intent on sharing his excitement, on getting everyone onside, that he barrels through without consideration, chopping out the empty spaces, the breaks of playful exercises that Mike and Jim had stressed were essential: downtime, play, the relaxation that leads to creative ideas. It's past five o'clock when Renada interrupts, "I have to leave in fifteen minutes." He knows this is not true. They would meet, like they always did on Thursdays after work, at the hotel on The Queensway. He stumbles a moment, smiles to stop himself from saying this out loud, stumbles enough to notice the room, the people, their faces hanging in boredom around the table, almost—he's almost sure of it—in hostility. It's a thickness in the room, something he'd been lassoing for the last two hours, teasing it into being as he spoke, oblivious to response. He stumbles, looks at this binder, his notes, the lists taped around the room, loose paper, bold and ragged print in blue and green and red. He feels the hostility now, coming from each person, flowing toward him as he spoke, banking so long around him, nudging up, washing in, in a circle around him, wave after wave pushing up against what he did not see, and it broke through, with his awareness, washed up around the charts, the lists, the pages of the binder he knew so well, washed under his enthusiasm, his drive, the coherence of his plan dissembled. He stumbled and recovered. "I've gone on too long," he says, pulling loose the knot of his tie. "Let's book a time for the next meet-ing." We pull out our daybooks, our calendars, and I try to do the same, but he has pulled off his tie.

He is standing there above us at the front of the room, blocking the door. Bright light behind him and my body cringes into freeze. Rigid. Sweat. Heat. Breath. Choke. He drags the knot down to the tie-end, pulls the band of material from around his neck, and holds it hand to hand, tugging it tight, thin, across his chest, thin as a rail, thin as leather, thin as a belt stretching across his body, blocking the door, the exit, the escape.

I am held there, by the belt, by his hands. We are numb, wretched. The people around me sit, drink, argue about the placement of desks and meetings. Inside my heart tenses into the basement, struggling against an assault, while I join in the discussion, aggressive, not knowing that I am fighting for my life, my voice here somehow believing that a meeting at two o'clock rather than three will somehow rescue me from the months of basement; now, here, where it is far too late, an expression of will, an assertion of choice that could somehow correct my last decision to visit the basement. I could somehow undo it, avoid it, unshape my life from its effect, and become what I had been; if everyone in the office would only understand the importance of an hour, a moment, a step.

Eventually I step back. Remember that an hour is an hour, a desk is a desk, know that I am wrong, see that half is leaking into half and another shard of terror is making its way out.

When I return the meeting is weeks gone, another in its place, and I sit, listening, discussing, watching the people around me. From snippets of coffee break, lunchtime—Mary's husband left with her sister, Jasmine's mother plying her with care, Renada's move from aunt to aunt—I place the actions of argument into each past, find the shape of response, influence, predictable now, from each and me, clear as a river. Catching a glimpse of each, I follow the undercurrents, silent, watching, discerning the motivation of the flow of words and argument, the push beneath the push.

Stained

Leaving the coffee shop for a day job is no easy matter. Allowing myself to sleep through the night when the night has been my life. So much solace there, so much peace in darkness.

When Max left to get the police, I waited, then crawled knee by knee, plank by plank into the air toward the girl. The ropes bulged round the planks and her and the girders, a complex system of hairy loops and tangles, almost flattened at the edges where the weight of her pulled it down. I whispered. I sang. I reached down to where her head hung back, placing my hands on her shoulders, her face, her neck, knowing a pulse would be there if there was one but not knowing how to find it. I stroked and patted and whispered. The blue wind drifted across us, winding around our bodies, cutting through the thin space between us until the warmth of our bodies created a peace. By and by I heard the crunch of gravel under wheels, the low drone of an engine above the wind. Mom and Dad came, and Max and Meg. Our pictures were all over the papers. You might remember.

On my last shift Margie calls her daughter Ann in and we have cream éclairs. She'll be graduating in June, accepted at college and university, still undecided about which, she thinks she may take a year off, work or travel. Her indecision weights her down, sends her dashing in

every direction, drives Margie mad with worry. I wonder what it's like, this weight of future, in the context of
safety, wonder what I might have become, what life is, to
children who never break like this, when they are small.
Is she more safe, more whole? Is life good outside of terror. Is she safe? I lick the last edge of powder cinnamon
from my fingers as an April snow, the last of the year, falls
in heavy flakes to the pavement.

To say that I'm happy would be incorrect but there's a
calm from reconciling myself to my past and what I became there, and it might be a kind of happiness to be
released from longing for dreams long dead. At some
points, often, it feels entirely stupid to have struggled
so desperately only to reach here, the ordinary. Such an
effort to survive only to come here, out of the spotlight
of devastation. Then it does feel like an awful joke. But
this is it, isn't it? Just being here where the day isn't falling apart or threatening to fall apart; where there's time
to do, and energy to do, some of the things that seemed
lost forever.

It was, I see, easy for me to feel I was doing well in
my small world, with Louis; easy for me to feel that I'd
accomplished something and that everything was in my
grasp. It hasn't been easy to get a sense of where I fit in
this larger place. I don't know if I might have made a good
enough life without the breakdown. It seems unlikely. If
things had continued with Louis—the job, marriage,
children, a steady stable life—without knowledge of my
most extreme experiences, I would be less. The terrible
sadness of losing what I was, knowing now that without
this loss there is no sense of the stretch of me, how far I
can go without dying, and return. This kind of life would

have been an act of terror, as much as an act of mind. It is better to know—not better, but more good.

I live now in a tiny house on the lake, a sliver of yard between slivers that line the shore, our houses protecting the lake from the street. The land is flat from the road to the house, the yard behind is level a few metres before it drops: in stairs or stones or a thin dirt path; drops metre by metre—the scent of water, of kelp, of fish—to the lip of the shore. How sweet is fresh water that comes across the ground from ice caps so far away; how sweet it is, to rush and flow and trickle from source to river to stream and become wide, this wide, wide as the human horizon can be without movement; a tilt of the head, turn of the body, that shifts everything. I sit at the bottom of the cliff, level to the basement. I can see his frailty now, Mr. Kennedy. I can see his failure. And the people around him, us, stronger, more able, turned away, as people do. As we do. It's a human frailty, this looking away. Once he came, sat in a corner, and cried and cried, calling *Mother, Mom.* I was pulled back into the room, back into my body, child body, holding a man twice my size, four times my age, becoming a woman as he shrunk and diminished into infancy, helpless. Even my heart, in the moment of attack, could not remain unaffected. It was the only time I responded, holding him. Placed my arms slightly, only slightly, around his shoulders, the impression of a caress emanating from my fingertips, a thought, just a thought, that we both knew. It was, and has been, my deepest connection, human to human: this brief and almost real flash-and-gone gesture of tenderness in the blaze of assault. It was nothing. Invisible. Unremarked. Unacknowledged. Things started to happen from there. I began asking only for chocolate bars, Sweet Maries, eating them voraciously, knowing he would have to buy carton after carton. I asked for tapes: Jackson Five, Bee Gees, Bay City Rollers. I asked for comic books, bubble gum, pink barrettes, and imagined him, helpless, unaware, going from store to store, leaving a trail of actions that would form a sentence, a language, that someone, somewhere, would hear: a stray thread of incongruity caught in the moment that stayed in the mind, dangling to the next action and the next until they joined and pointed to a man, a house, to a door I had walked through a lifetime before.

I walk down the slope, a long loose loping of arms and legs, spine curved swaying, balancing against the push of gravity but using it, too, to come down the embankment. I carry a black straw bag with a blanket, muffins and fruit, and make a picnic on a rock. I can feel in myself, what Mr. Kennedy pushed into me there, the piece of himself that he could not bear or overcome. It sleeps in me here, this morning, and will sleep for days, months, maybe even years, but it is a puncture, a tear, in the fabric of what I am, a force hidden under the routine, smiles, pleasantries, shaping what I want and what I can and cannot do. I remember Louis; feel now, more than a decade later, the warmth of his hands on my skin, my belly churning; remember the distance of touch, my coldness on the other side of memory. How could we not see it, sense it, when he held me, when we walked, when we lived together day by day for eight years. How can two bodies come so close without touching? But there's that lens there, the one that gets lost to mind, that disk of near-light, shifted sideways, that I held in place for as long as I could, not wanting to let it go, small girl, peaking around the side, waiting for someone—a voice, a hand, a home—to speak one sigh and knock it sideways, shattered, once and for all.

Not shattered, though, not shattered. But placed in the heap along with all the other discarded wishes. What we know, what we wish were true. Louis's lens was so strong, so firmly placed, he would never have conceived another. Strange how deep it goes, how firmly embedded.

And, for me, I cannot get rid of a longing for death. It stays beside me, snuffling around my knees, paws on my shoulders, licking my face when the nights are too long. Then down again, sauntering beside my knees.

Stripped down, in darkness, of illusion and effect, I became a stone, still conscious. One day the door opened and I was let out but it was too late. I had already seen it, and it freezes the soul; lays there at the bottom of will and being, a dead part now at the core, paralyzed for the terror of knowing oneself to be abandoned by god.

I have seen the sun, backwards, and cannot unsee.

So that, when they came one day, finally, I was already dead. If I bobbed up like a cork into life, and smiled and laughed, made love and plans, had sex and jobs and continued on; however vital and integral a shell I became, however thick, complex, passionate, the seed was gone, empty, hollow. It was too late; it was an illusion. In the basement, in the darkness, night after night after night until day became night and life became death, there was no Magda to save. And I am ashamed.

You hear something different here. You hear an echo that needed to become a source.

Sometimes the echo is enormous, as if I have seen and been everything that living is, and, sometimes, that only I can see all the layers of perception that overlay the core of what we are. Sometimes—more enormous still—that each of us has all of this, knows all of it, held in silence, not dormant but carrying.

Sometimes the echo is small, more wretched than a broken kitten mewling in a cold alley, unheard. In this, too, there is humanity. Maybe more so.

How each thought can become an entire world. Mostly I navigate a perception that shifts and heaves under the flow of urban courtesies, necessities, rudeness; ice-block memory bloating up; emergent sway tipping up against alarm clock, bus stop, task done, grocery bag, repeat. Holding out, still, to the gravitational turn of the earth, a physics larger than me, that brings light/ starlight/ dawn unfailing, keeping our small bodies pinned to the blue earth, gentle as breathing the next breath.

The sun is just setting in Vancouver now, rising in Kyoto; night is moving across Canada into the Pacific as sunrise comes to Hong Kong, Istanbul, Cairo, London. The entire expanse of Eurasia holding daylight for a breath before dusk creeps in, softening, pushing us into dawn, another day. Light. The blue curtain lifts in the wind, high into the room, lands across my body. The air is damp with lake and rain; my body damp with sweat. My body churns with memory, sparks in quivering in waves. Desire flushes an involuntary surge, like biting a lemon but in sweetness, in heat.

Where we approach each other, where we touch, it feels that the molecules of our bodies have softened and mingled, as close as the sounds we've shared, the thoughts, actions. In the theory of light two quarks, once in relation, remain mutually responsive, despite the distance of space and time. Are we not as much as any quark? When once an action occurs, there's no disappearing. I know this now in the actions of terror, and begin to get a sense of it here in the actions of love. There are places on my skin that had only been touched by my mother, my dad. Their soft hands on my baby belly. It was the only memory my body held until he put his life there harsh and hard. Undoing these actions from my skin is slow work. But Carson is there, as my mother's hands were there, and Dana, Louis. Cell memory layered on the other side of violence, years of touch kindly stroking and soothing through the ice, the burn.

I stand with my hands immersed in hot soapy water, looking out over the yard, the lake. The moon rises in the east, round and orange and huge, more close than it has been in a hundred years. The orbit of the earth has its warp, its larger rhythms, and today we are closer to the sun than we will be for another hundred years. Haley's comet streaked the sky last year for a week or so. Bits of evidence, clues to a broader life. The moment passes. The trajectory steadies, becomes lost to sight. What is it that holds us here? That holds the sun?

There is a woman tied up over the ravine, the long rail stretched into blue, dot of land on the other side. Slat and slat and slat. I stand here. She is there. I kneel here. My palms and knees balance on the rough wood. Stones nip the tops of my feet. I have bitten a hole in my lip, white teeth piercing red, rust in my dry mouth. I shift my weight off a hand and a knee, onto a hand and a knee, and inch forward. One slat, two slat. The stones disappear. The land disappears. Stop here where the wood and rail continues but the ground does not. Listen to my breath, my heart. She is there. Move forward, into the blue.

Sometimes memory has no choice. I do not know if there is good here, but that a truth persists whether we walk away or go back. An echo in the dark, held by waves, by light.

Acknowledgements

The author acknowledges with gratitude the support of The Ontario Arts Council and The Canada Council for the Arts. Particular gratitude goes to the Canadian writing community for a vitality and richness fondly exasperating to hermits, and for the care and comments of writers who read early drafts, including Sheila, Antje, Andre' and Elise.

The larger section headings are after books that may be evoked in the sections, which were of great use and comfort to me through the years.

Canadian Pastoral, after Philip Roth's *American Pastoral*
General Linguistics, after Ferdinand de Saussure's *A Course in General Linguistics*
Affliction, Russell Banks
If This is a Woman, after Primo Levi's *If This is a Man*
The Metamorphosis, Franz Kafka
Of A Common Language, after Adrienne Rich's *The Dream of a Common Language*
Light, after Elie Wiesel's *Night*
A Bridge, Not an End, after Nietzsche's *"Humanity is a rope, tied between the beast and the Overman – a rope over an abyss. What is great in humanity is that we are a bridge and not an end…"*
A Beautiful Mind, Sylvia Nasar's biography of John Nash
Wave Rider, after John Brunner's *Shockwave Rider*

The Invisible Woman, after Ralph Ellison, *The Invisible Man*

The Art of Maintenance, after Robert M. Pirsig's *Zen and the Art of Motorcycle Maintenance*

Wake Again, somewhat after James Joyce's *Finnegans Wake*, but more a nod to Modernists in general, from Woolf to Kerouac to Kincaid

Solitude, Anthony Storr

Stained, after Philip Roth's *The Human Stain*

About the Author

Elizabeth Ukrainetz grew up in Toronto, Canada, where she works as a clerk. She accidentally kept re-reading Kaufman's *Portable Nietzsche* for five years, before encountering the larger world of abstraction at York University. After earning a B.A. in Fine Arts Studies, she discovered a knack for language and has been writing since, trying to reconcile the particularities of personal experience to the world at large. She writes both prose and poetry, and has published regularly across Canada, including two books: *Baby I Love You* and *Minor Assumptions*.